Archibald Henry Sayce

The Life and Times of Isaiah

Archibald Henry Sayce

The Life and Times of Isaiah

ISBN/EAN: 9783337054250

Printed in Europe, USA, Canada, Australia, Japan

Cover: Foto ©Raphael Reischuk / pixelio.de

More available books at **www.hansebooks.com**

By-Paths of Bible Knowledge.

XIII.

THE

LIFE AND TIMES OF ISAIAH

AS ILLUSTRATED BY CONTEMPORARY MONUMENTS.

BY

A. H. SAYCE, LL.D.

AUTHOR OF
'FRESH LIGHT FROM THE MONUMENTS,'
'THE HITTITES, OR THE STORY OF A FORGOTTEN EMPIRE,' ETC.

THE RELIGIOUS TRACT SOCIETY,

56 PATERNOSTER ROW, 65 ST. PAUL'S CHURCHYARD,

AND 164 PICCADILLY.

1889

PREFACE.

— •• —

IN the following pages an attempt has been made to bring before the modern reader a picture of the external and internal politics of the Jewish kingdom in the age of Isaiah, one of the most important epochs and turning-points in the religious history and training of the Chosen Race. The materials for drawing such a picture are derived partly from the Old Testament, partly from the monuments of Egypt and Assyria, which in these our days have thrown so vivid and unexpected a light upon the earlier history of the Bible. Without them, indeed, the present book could never have been written. It is with their assistance that the pages of the sacred record have been supplemented and illustrated, and the course of events which seemed such a puzzle to the scholars of a former generation has been traced in its broad outlines. The contemporaries of Isaiah have ceased to be mere names to us, and have become living men of flesh and blood ; we can not only read the very words of Tiglath-pileser, of Sargon, and of Sennacherib, but even handle the very documents which they caused to be inscribed. We can sit at the councils of the Assyrian kings and follow the reasons which brought them into contact with the rulers of Judah. A world which had seemed hopelessly past and dead has in the good providence of God been suddenly quickened into life.

It was inevitable that in this reconstruction of the past we should have to modify or renounce many theories and interpretations of Holy Writ which have long prevailed in default of better knowledge. It was so when modern astronomy swept away the old theory which placed the earth in the centre of the universe; it was equally so when geology showed that the earth was far older than had hitherto been believed. All new knowledge necessarily obliges us to correct and modify our earlier conceptions; and nowhere is this more the case than in the domain of history, where too often the chain of events that has been preserved for us consists only of a few broken links.

There is one point in particular in which the inscriptions of Assyria have come to the aid of the student of the Old Testament Scriptures. The chronology of the later kings of Samaria and the contemporary Kings of Judah has long been the despair of the historian. Rival schemes of chronology have been put forward, each claiming to be the only accurate or possible one. Interregna have been invented for which there is no warrant in the Books of Kings, and texts have been combined or dissociated from one another according to the fancy of the writer. The decipherment of the cuneiform tablets has at last set the question at rest.

The Assyrians kept a strict chronological register by means of certain officers called *limmi* or 'eponymes.' The eponyme was changed each year, the years being named after the several eponymes who presided over them. Lists of these eponymes have been discovered, and consequently a continuous chronological table exists which extends from the tenth to the middle of the seventh century B.C. The date of a king's accession is always recorded, and in some of the lists the principal events which marked the years are mentioned. As the Assyrian kings were careful to give the names of the eponymes who presided over the different years in which the events they record took place, we can now determine exactly, not only the date of the accession of a Tiglath-pileser or the death of an Esar-haddon, but also the year in which Sennacherib invaded Judah, or Menahem of Samaria paid tribute to his Assyrian lord.

The conquest of Judah by Sargon ten years before the invasion of Sennacherib is another instance of the unexpected light which the Assyrian inscriptions have cast upon the pages of the Old Testament. The difficulties presented by the tenth and twenty-second chapters of the Book of Isaiah have been removed, as well as the apparent inconsistencies in the account given by the sacred historian of the campaign of Sennacherib against Hezekiah. A full discussion of this point, however, belongs to a critical introduction to the text of Isaiah rather than to a description of the age in which the prophet lived, and those who wish to study it may do so in Canon Cheyne's well-known Commentary upon Isaiah. But the present work will show how important the historical fact is to a full understanding of the political circumstances of Hezekiah's reign.

Unfortunately the annals of Sargon have reached us in too imperfect a state to furnish us with the details of his campaign in Judah. Future excavations in Assyria may fill up the imperfections of the record, and allow us to trace the march of the Assyrian army towards the gates of Jerusalem. Meanwhile we must be grateful for what the discoveries and research of the nineteenth century have already given us. All good and perfect gifts come to us from the Father of Lights, and not the least has been the resurrection of that ancient Oriental world in the midst of which the Jewish Church was being prepared and fitted for the day when the true Light should come into the world and tabernacle among us.

A. H. SAYCE.

TABLE OF CONTENTS.

———— •• ————

CHRONOLOGY.

B. C.

756. Jotham made regent along with his father Uzziah.

745. April. Pul usurps the Assyrian throne, taking the title of Tiglath-pileser III.

742. Uzziah sends help to Hamath ; death of Uzziah.

741. Death of Jotham and accession of Ahaz.

738. Tribute paid to the Assyrians by Menahem and Rezon.

734. Damascus besieged : the tribes beyond the Jordan carried away ; Jehoahaz or Ahaz becomes an Assyrian vassal.

732. Damascus captured ; Rezon put to death ; Ahaz at Damascus.

730. Pekah put to death and succeeded by Hoshea.

727. Tiglath-pileser succeeded by Shalmaneser IV. and Ahaz by Hezekiah.

722. Sargon seizes the throne and captures Samaria.

721. Merodach-baladan conquers Babylon.

712-11. Embassy of Merodach-baladan to Hezekiah.

711. Conquest of Judah and Ashdod by Sargon.

710. Conquest of Babylonia by Sargon.

705. Sargon murdered and succeeded by his son Sennacherib.

701. Sennacherib's campaign against Judah ; battle of Eltekeh : retreat of the Assyrians.

697. Death of Hezekiah and accession of his son Manasseh.

681. Sennacherib murdered and succeeded by his son Esar-haddon.

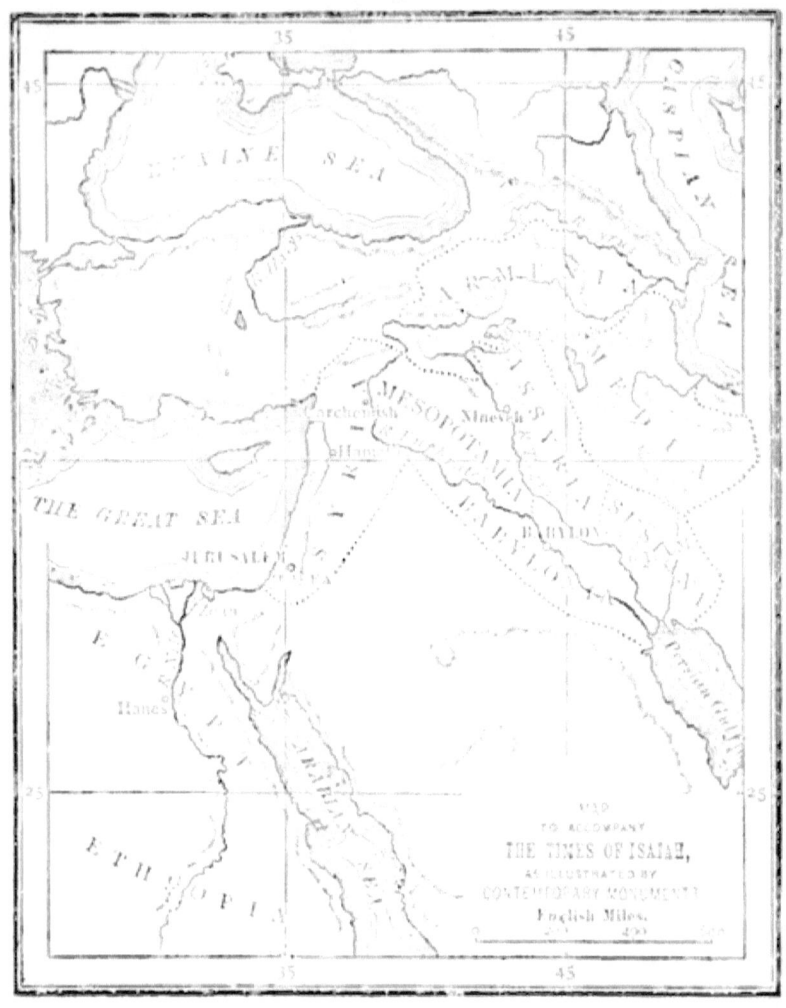

CHAPTER I.

AMONG all the prophets of the Old Testament there is none who holds a more prominent place than Isaiah, the son of Amoz. It has been said of him that he died with the Gospel on his lips. Nowhere can we find the promise of the Messiah more clearly announced; nowhere is the kingdom of the Messiah depicted in colours more lifelike and abiding. The prophetic vision of Isaiah is not restricted by the narrow limits of his age and country; he sees the Church of Christ rising before him and uniting in one the Jew and the Gentile. The day should come, he declared, when Egypt and Assyria, the representatives of the unbelieving powers of the world, should join with Israel in adoring the one true God, when the Lord of Hosts should say of them, 'Blessed be Egypt My people, and Assyria the work of My hands.' The prophecies of Isaiah form, as it were, a bridge between the Old Covenant and the New.

But there are other respects besides this in which Isaiah occupies a foremost place among the Hebrew prophets. The old times were passing away, when the prophet appealed to the eye rather han to the ear and the mind. The symbolical actions through which the will of God was made known to His people were replaced by solemn warnings, or promises of forgiveness. It is true that the glowing words of the prophet might still at

times be accompanied by some visible action, as when
Isaiah 'walked naked and barefoot three years for a sign
and wonder upon Egypt and upon Ethiopia;' but such
visible actions were accompaniments only, and tended to
disappear altogether. The prophet became in very truth
a *prophêtês* or 'announcer' of the will of God to man.
The miracles, by which an Elijah or an Elisha had attested
their power and the truth of their mission, made way for
the more spiritual testimony of prophecy itself. The
range of the prophet's vision was no longer confined to
his own nation and people; the message he delivered
was addressed to other nations as well. In Isaiah, therefore, we see prophecy increasing in evangelical clearness,
in spirituality, and in catholicity. It embraces all men,
not the chosen people only, and promises to Jew and
Gentile alike the blessings of the Messianic kingdom.

Isaiah himself held a position suitable to the message
he was commissioned to announce. He was not an un-
taught man like Amos, who had been taken by the Lord
while following the flock (Am. vii. 14, 15), but an educated
student from the prophetic schools, whose prophecies
show full acquaintance with the literature of the past,
and who shared in that revival of culture and learning
which seems to have marked the reign of Hezekiah.
Nay, more than this. He was the councillor and adviser
of kings, a statesman who took a keen interest in the
politics of his day, and to whose efforts, under divine
instruction, Jerusalem was indebted for the successful
defence it made against the armies of Sennacherib.
During the reign of Hezekiah, at any rate, Isaiah was
held in high honour; the policy he had urged was proved
by events to be the only right one, and Judah for a while
seemed willing to walk in the path of reformation.

His lot was happier than that which fell usually to the Hebrew prophet. He was not called upon to see his threatenings and remonstrances wholly thrown away and neglected, or his countrymen blindly rushing upon the doom of which they were warned in vain; on the contrary, the reforms of Hezekiah gave practical effect to Isaiah's preaching, and after the lesson taught by the invasion and overthrow of Sennacherib that policy of 'rest' and dependence on God, which he had so long proclaimed[1], seems to have prevailed up to the time of Hezekiah's death.

In spite, however, of the influence he exercised upon his contemporaries, our knowledge of Isaiah's life is derived for the most part from his own works. It is true that he comes before us in the Book of Kings as the councillor to whom the Jewish monarch and his ministers betook themselves in their hour of need, as the prophet who was empowered to promise them a speedy deliverance, as the healer who restored Hezekiah to life when all earthly hope of recovery seemed gone, and finally as the stern reprover of the monarch's pride and worldliness. But the passages in which Isaiah is thus brought before us are found also in the book that bears his name: the only additional information we receive is the record in the Second Book of Chronicles (xxxii. 32) that 'the rest of the acts of Hezekiah, and his goodness, behold, they are written in the vision of Isaiah the prophet, the son of Amoz.'

The name of his father Amoz has been associated by Rabbinical ingenuity with that of the Jewish king Amaziah, whose brother he is supposed to have been. But, apart from chronological difficulties, it does not seem probable that Isaiah was closely connected with the royal family.

[1] Is. xxx. 15.

In 2 Kings xx. 4 it is stated that when Isaiah left the
royal palace to return to his own house 'he went out of
the middle city,' though the Authorised Version gives a
different sense to the Hebrew words. As the palace
stood between the temple on Mount Moriah and the
lower city, in which the mass of the inhabitants of
Jerusalem dwelt, we may conclude that his course lay
towards the lower and not the upper town, and that here
he lived among the ordinary citizens of Jerusalem. It is
not necessary to point out the further improbability that
two brothers should have borne what is practically the
same name, Amoz '(He is) strong.' and Amaziah 'The
Lord (is) strong.' If we are to connect the names at all,
we must make them one and the same[1].

Isaiah's own name signifies 'The salvation of the Lord.'
It was thus, as he himself tells us, that he was a 'sign
and wonder in Israel from the Lord of Hosts,' like his
children, whose names were equally ever-present witnesses
of the prophecies he had uttered[2]. The constant burden
of his preaching had been that though the heathen should
rage for awhile against Judah, though the tree of the
chosen people should be felled to the root, God would
yet have mercy upon it; the root should again put forth
its shoots, 'a remnant' should return and behold the
'salvation of the Lord[3].' His own name was as surely
a token of forgiveness to repentant Judah as was the
name of his son Shear-jashub, 'a remnant shall return.'

Shear-jashub was perhaps the eldest of his children.
He was, at all events, old enough to accompany his father
when he went out of the city to meet Ahaz, who was

---

[1] A Hebrew seal inscribed with characters of earlier date than the period
of the Exile, and now in the possession of Dr. Grant of Cairo, contains the
name of 'Amoz the scribe.'

[2] Is. viii. 18.   [3] Is. vi. 13, x. 20-22, xii. 2, xxvi. 1.

examining 'the conduit of the upper pool' at the beginning of the Syro-Ephraimitic war [1]. At a later date was
born Maher-shalal-hash-baz, 'spoil swiftly, rob quickly.'
These were the words Isaiah had been ordered to write
on a 'large slab,' with 'the graving-tool of the people'
(Is. viii. 1), so that all might see and read, and then to
give them as a name to the child that was born to
him shortly afterwards. The name, like the inscription,
was to be a sign that 'before the child shall have knowledge to cry, My father, and my mother, the riches of
Damascus and the spoil of Samaria shall be taken away
before the king of Assyria.'

The wife of Isaiah is termed 'the prophetess.' From
this we must infer that she also, like her husband, was
endowed with the gift of prophecy. The usage of Hebrew
would not allow us to interpret the title as we might
perhaps in English, where it could signify simply a
prophet's wife.

Isaiah seems to have lived to a fair old age. The
superscription of his prophecies tells us that he saw
his 'vision concerning Judah and Jerusalem in the days
of Uzziah, Jotham, Ahaz, and Hezekiah.' The late
Jewish legend, accordingly, which maintained that he
had been sawn asunder by Manasseh, must be rejected.
Such a mode of death was of Persian invention, while the
legend runs counter to the plain sense of the superscription. We may feel assured that Isaiah was spared the
pain of witnessing the overthrow of Hezekiah's reforms
and the idolatries of Manasseh's reign. The 'vision' or
revelation vouchsafed to him did not extend beyond
Hezekiah's lifetime; the prophet, it would seem, had
passed away before the godless son had succeeded to

[1] Is. vii. 3.

his father's throne. His ministry had lasted through the reigns of four Jewish kings, beginning, as we may infer, from the words of vi. 1, 'in the year that king Uzziah died.'

The chronology of this period of Jewish history, so long the despair of chronologists, has now been settled by the help of the Assyrian records. It was in B.C. 742 that Azariah or Uzziah, according to the Assyrian king, Tiglath-pileser III, encouraged the people of Hamath to resist the Assyrian monarch ; in B.C. 734 Tiglath-pileser received the tribute and submission of Ahaz, and in B.C. 701 Sennacherib made his attack upon Hezekiah which ended so fatally for the invading host. We may therefore conclude that Isaiah's public ministry extended over a period of between forty and fifty years, and if he were more than twenty years of age when he was consecrated to it, he would have been past sixty when he laid it down. Such a length of life does not, it is true, seem very great to us in these days of advanced medical knowledge and sanitary arrangements, but it was beyond the average age of Isaiah's contemporaries. Ahaz was only thirty-six when he died, Hezekiah fifty-four, and the 90th Psalm tells us that ' the days of our years are threescore years and ten.' If Isaiah was sixty-five when he died, he would already have been looked upon as an old man.

It is probable that Isaiah published his prophecies in separate collections or volumes. They are not arranged in chronological order. It is not until we come to the sixth chapter that we read the account of his appointment to his prophetic office. It has been supposed that some at least of the preceding chapters belong to the reign of Jotham. The first chapter forms a whole by itself, the next four relate to the same subject—the calamities that await Jerusalem for its sins—and are prefaced by a quotation from some older prophet which begins with the conjunction 'and' (ii. 2, comp. Mic. iv. 1). The prophecies against foreign nations are grouped together by the common 'burden' with which they begin, just as a later series of prophecies (xxviii–xxxiii.) are connected by the denunciation of 'woe' by which they are prefaced. It is possible that the historical chapters (xxxvi–xxxix.) are an extract from 'the vision,' which, as we learn from the Books of Chronicles, embodied the history of Hezekiah; though here again, as we shall see later on, there is no chronological arrangement, the account of Sennacherib's invasion, which took place ten years after the embassy of Merodach-Baladan, being narrated first.

Many of the prophecies were delivered orally before they were committed to writing, but others, such as those directed against foreign nations, must have been written down from the first. The prophet would have used a scroll of leather or papyrus, and the limits of each collection of his prophecies would have been determined by the size of the scroll. We may suppose that in successive editions of them he united these collections together, until finally the book was formed, such as we now have it. In arranging the several collections, regard was had to the subject-matter of each rather than to their strict chronological order; hence it is that the history of Isaiah's consecration to the prophetic office is not placed at the beginning of the book, and that prophecies like that upon Egypt, which belongs to the later portion of the prophet's life, precede the account of the sign given 'in the year when the Tartan' or commander-in-chief of Sargon came against Ashdod in 711 B.C.

The selections made from the history of Hezekiah's reign, which are incorporated into the volume of prophecies, owe their position in it to the fact that they contain the predictions and words of Isaiah. The invasion of Judah by Sennacherib led to the prophecy in which the Lord declared that He would humble the insolent pride of the Assyrian monarch, and would defend His city of Jerusalem; while the account of Hezekiah's sickness and of the Babylonian embassy embody the promise made through Isaiah that God would deliver Jerusalem out of the hand of the king of Assyria, as well as the prediction that the day would come when the treasures of the royal palace would be carried away to Babylon. However much we may regret that the rest of the history of Hezekiah has been lost, it is clear that no other prophecies of Isaiah were contained in it. Had they been so, they would have been included in 'the vision of Isaiah the son of Amoz.'

THE life of Isaiah fell in an age which was a momentous one for the kingdom of Judah. Judah had become the battle-ground of the two great powers of the ancient world, Assyria and Egypt. While Isaiah was still a boy, Assyria had suddenly awakened to new life and energy, and had begun to push its conquests towards the west. Syria, and even the northern kingdom of Israel, had been swept away, and Judah found itself face to face with a seemingly irresistible empire. To the south, the desert, into which the fertile plains of Southern Judæa imperceptibly passed, touched upon the borders of Egypt. Like the iron upon the anvil, therefore, Judah lay between two hostile forces, one of which was burning with the youthful fires of enterprise and lust of conquest, while the other still remembered its former glories and the empire it had wielded in Asia.

For Egypt had once been mistress, not only of Palestine, but of Northern Syria also as far as the Euphrates and the Gulf of Antioch. This was in the far-off days when as yet the Israelites had not entered the promised land, when they were still groaning under the Egyptian oppressor. But the oppression had been fearfully avenged. Hardly had Ramses II, the Pharaoh of the Oppression, died, when the empire he had founded passed away. Egypt was herself attacked by the enemy, and while rival princes were founding dynasties in different parts of the country, the cities were sacked and burned by savage marauders, and the people were compelled to bow the neck to kings of foreign race. For a time, indeed, under Shishak I, the despoiler of Jerusalem (1 Kings xiv. 25), the Egyptian armies went forth again to conquer; but Shishak himself was not an Egyptian by birth, and the line of sovereigns he founded soon became as feeble as the dynasties that had preceded them. By the middle of the eighth century B.C. the land was once more divided among a number of hostile princes whose power did not extend far beyond the limits of the cities in which they had established themselves. Their petty jealousies and constant quarrels opened the road to the invader; then, as now, the weakness of Egypt was the opportunity of the tribes of the south: and Ethiopian armies marched out of the Soudân, to burn, to slay, and to plunder.

An end was put to this condition of things by the Ethiopian king Shabaka, or Sabako. He is the So of the Old Testament (2 Kings xvii. 4), whom Hoshea had bribed to help him against the Assyrian monarch. But before that help could be sent the Assyrian had descended on his rebellious vassal, whom he dethroned and imprisoned. Now, as ever, the Egyptian had proved to be a 'bruised reed' to those who trusted in him.

Sabako, in fact, was too much engaged in consolidating his power in Egypt to think of foreign conquests. He had overthrown the representative of the Egyptian royal family, and, if we may believe the statement of a classical writer, had burned him alive. It took him some time to put down the various princes who claimed sovereignty over different parts of Egypt, to crush all opposition to himself among the Egyptian people, and to weld together his Egyptian and Ethiopian possessions. The task was rendered easier by the fact that Sabako, though king of Ethiopia and leader of the Ethiopian forces, was not altogether of Ethiopian blood. He claimed descent from the ancient royal line of Egypt. When the feeble successors of the great Ramses had allowed the provinces of the Soudân to be torn from their grasp, and the highpriests of the god of Thebes eventually to dispossess them of the throne, some of their descendants had fled to the south, and there at Napata, under the shadow of the Holy Mountain, the modern Gebel Barkal, had established a kingdom which was in all respects the counterpart of the old kingdom of Egypt. Not only were the sovereigns themselves Egyptians, their court was Egyptian also, speaking the Egyptian language, and following Egyptian customs. By degrees, however, the influence of the land over which they ruled began to make itself felt. The kings and nobles of Meroe became less and less Egyptian in blood, in language, and in manners. In the age of Sabako, nevertheless, the Egyptian element was still strong, and it was consequently not difficult for him to assume the character of an Egyptian monarch, or for the Egyptian people to regard him as one of themselves.

Under Sabako and his successors, therefore, the Egyptians and the Ethiopians were under the same sceptre, and looked upon themselves as a single nation. Hence it is that 'Pharaoh, king of Egypt,' in whom, according to the Assyrian Rab-shakeh, Hezekiah put his confidence, is described later on as 'Tirhakah, king of Ethiopia [1]'; hence too it is that Isaiah declares that

[1] Is. xxxvi. 6, xxxvii. 9.

the Assyrian king shall 'lead away the Egyptians prisoners, and the Ethiopians captives,' and that the Jewish people shall ' be ashamed of Ethiopia their expectation, and of Egypt their glory[1].' But with all this fusion of the two populations the position of Sabako was by no means secure. The Egyptians, more especially the aristocratic portion of them, could not forget that he was a foreigner and a conqueror, even though he might trace his lineage from their own ancient race of kings. He was therefore necessarily prevented from pursuing a policy of foreign conquest; his energies were fully employed in stamping out the seeds of disaffection at home, and he could waste neither men nor time in invasions of Asia. He might receive the presents sent by Hoshea, but he was not in any hurry to make the return Hoshea expected.

Before his death, however, he was forced to cross arms with the Assyrians. The Assyrian king did not forget that the rebels of Israel and Hamath had been encouraged by promises of support from Egypt. In B.C. 720, accordingly, after the fall of Samaria, Sargon, the Assyrian monarch, led his forces to the south of Judah, and at Raonia, on the road to Egypt, met the allied army of Sabako and the Philistines of Gaza. The Assyrians gained a complete victory, the result of which was the capture of Gaza, and the end of all Egyptian interference for awhile in the affairs of Palestine. In B.C. 711, it is true, when a revolt had broken out there against the Assyrians, the rebels believed that they would be assisted by the Egyptian monarch; but so far was this from being the case, that after the suppression of the revolt ' the king of Meroe' delivered up to Sargon

[1] Is. xx. 4, 5.

one of the leaders of the outbreak who had fled into Egypt.

The immediate successor of Sabako does not seem to have reigned long ; at any rate, he continued the policy of his predecessor. But on his death, Tirhakah (Taharka), brother-in-law of Sabako, came to the throne, and soon entered upon a new line of action. Whether he thought that the Ethiopian domination was now too firmly established in Egypt to be shaken, or that it was necessary at all hazards to oppose the growing power of Assyria, we do not know ; certain it is that under Tirhakah the Egyptians and Ethiopians once more began to turn their eyes to Palestine, and to intermeddle with its politics.

Assyria had suddenly become formidable. The kingdoms of Damascus and Samaria had been destroyed and placed under an Assyrian satrap ; Phœnicia, Judah, and the Philistines paid tribute to Nineveh ; and the authority of the Assyrian king was acknowledged as far south as the frontiers of Egypt. Between Assyria on the one side and Egypt on the other, the little kingdom of Judah alone remained in a semi-independent state.

The almost impregnable fortress of Jerusalem, which stood within it, gave it an importance which its small size and want of resources would not otherwise have justified. It is true that the hostile armies of Egypt and Assyria might turn the flank of Jerusalem by marching along the sea-coast ; but as long as such a fortress was left unoccupied it was difficult, if not impossible, for either power to retain a firm hold on the country north or south. An Assyrian army, when engaged in an invasion of Egypt, might always be attacked in the rear from Jerusalem, while an Egyptian army which had reached Phœnicia could always be prevented from returning

home.   Only by the possession or the submission of
Jerusalem could the Assyrians feel safe when attacking
Egypt, or the Egyptians when marching northward
towards Syria and the Euphrates.   The power which
wished to dominate over Western Asia had first to assure
itself of the help or neutrality of the capital of Judah.

Judah was consequently in the position of Bulgaria or
Afghanistan to-day.   It formed what has been termed 'a
buffer-state,' and its chances of safety seemed to lie in
playing Egypt and Assyria off one against the other.
Alternately threatened and cajoled by the two great
rival powers of the world, its statesmen leaned sometimes
to the one, sometimes to the other.   Egypt was the
nearest at hand, and its ancient *prestige*, the memory of
its former conquests in Palestine, and the maritime
intercourse between the Delta and Joppa, then as now
the port of Jerusalem, appeared to point it out as the
power that was the most formidable, and therefore most
necessary to be appeased.   But, on the other hand, the
Jews could not forget that only lately Egypt had been
in a condition of helplessness and anarchy, and that even
now it was governed by foreign conquerors ; while the
rapid advance of Assyria, and the ease with which the
Assyrian armies had swept away all that had stood in
their path, made the name of the Assyrian king a name
of terror to every inhabitant of Palestine.

The object of Tirhakah was, accordingly, to form a
league against Assyria in Palestine, of which Jerusalem
should be the head.

The course of events can be clearly traced from
Isaiah xxx. and Isaiah xviii, which we here quote in full
from the Revised Version : —

Woe to the rebellious children, saith the Lord, that take counsel, but not of Me ; and that cover with a covering, but not of My spirit, that they may add sin to sin : that walk to go down into Egypt, and have not asked at My mouth ; to strengthen themselves in the strength of Pharaoh, and to trust in the shadow of Egypt ! Therefore shall the strength of Pharaoh be your shame, and the trust in the shadow of Egypt your confusion. For his princes are at Zoan, and his ambassadors are come to Hanes. They shall all be ashamed of a people that cannot profit them, that are not an help nor profit, but a shame, and also a reproach.

The burden of the beasts of the South.

Through the land of trouble and anguish, from whence come the lioness and the lion, the viper and fiery flying serpent, they carry their riches upon the shoulders of young asses, and their treasures upon the bunches of camels, to a people that shall not profit them. For Egypt helpeth in vain, and to no purpose : therefore have I called her Rahab that sitteth still. Now go, write it before them on a tablet, and inscribe it in a book, that it may be for the time to come for ever and ever. For it is a rebellious people, lying children, children that will not hear the law of the Lord : which say to the seers, See not ; and to the prophets, Prophesy not unto us right things, speak unto us smooth things, prophesy deceits : get you out of the way, turn aside out of the path, cause the Holy One of Israel to cease from before us. Wherefore thus saith the Holy One of Israel, Because ye despise this word, and trust in oppression and perverseness, and stay thereon ; therefore this iniquity shall be to you as a breach ready to fall, swelling out in a high wall, whose breaking cometh suddenly at an instant. And he shall break it as a potter's vessel is broken, breaking it in pieces without sparing ; so that there shall not be found among the pieces thereof a sherd to take fire from the hearth, or to take water withal out of the cistern. For thus saith the Lord God, the Holy One of Israel, In returning and rest shall ye be saved ; in quietness and in confidence shall be your strength : and ye would not. But ye said, No, for we will flee upon horses ; therefore shall ye flee : and, We will ride upon the swift ; therefore shall they that pursue you be swift. One thousand shall flee at the rebuke of one ; at the rebuke of five shall ye flee : till ye be left as a beacon upon the top of a mountain, and as an ensign on an hill. And therefore will the Lord wait, that He may be gracious unto you, and therefore will He be exalted, that He may have mercy upon you : for the Lord is a God of judgement; blessed are all they that wait for Him.

For the people shall dwell in Zion at Jerusalem : thou shalt weep no more ; He will surely be gracious unto thee at the voice of thy cry: when He shall hear, He will answer thee. And though the Lord give you the bread of adversity and the water of affliction, yet shall not thy teachers be hidden any more, but thine eyes shall see thy teachers : and thine ears shall hear a word behind thee, saying, This is the way, walk ye in it : when ye turn to the right hand, and when ye turn to the left. And ye shall defile the over-laying of thy graven images of silver, and the plating of thy molten images of gold : thou shalt cast them away as an unclean thing : thou shalt say unto it, Get thee hence. And He shall give the rain of thy seed, that thou shalt sow the ground withal ; and bread of the increase of the ground, and it shall be fat and plenteous : in that day shall thy cattle feed in large pastures. The oxen likewise and the young asses that till the ground shall eat savoury provender, which hath been winnowed with the shovel and with the fan. And there shall be upon every lofty mountain, and upon every high hill, rivers and streams of waters, in the day of the great slaughter, when the towers fall. Moreover the light of the moon shall be as the light of the sun, and the light of the sun shall be sevenfold, as the light of seven days, in the day that the Lord bindeth up the hurt of His people, and healeth the stroke of their wound.

Behold, the name of the Lord cometh from far, burning with His anger, and in thick rising smoke : His lips are full of indignation, and His tongue is as a devouring fire : and His breath is as an overflowing stream, that reacheth even unto the neck, to sift the nations with the sieve of vanity : and a bridle that causeth to err shall be in the jaws of the peoples. Ye shall have a song as in the night when a holy feast is kept : and gladness of heart, as when one goeth with a pipe to come into the mountain of the Lord, to the Rock of Israel. And the Lord shall cause His glorious voice to be heard, and shall shew the lighting down of His arm, with the indignation of His anger, and the flame of a devouring fire, with a blast, and tempest, and hailstones. For through the voice of the Lord shall the Assyrian be broken in pieces, which smote with a rod. And every stroke of the appointed staff, which the Lord shall lay upon him, shall be with tabrets and harps : and in battles of shaking will He fight with them. For a Topheth is prepared of old ; yea, for the king it is made ready ; He hath made it deep and large : the pile thereof is fire and much wood ; the breath of the Lord, like a stream of brimstone, doth kindle it.

Ah, the land of the rustling of wings, which is beyond the rivers of Ethiopia : that sendeth ambassadors by the sea, even in vessels of papyrus upon the waters, saying, Go, ye swift messengers, to a nation tall and smooth, to a people terrible from their beginning onward : a nation that meteth out and treadeth down, whose land the rivers divide ! All ye inhabitants of the world, and ye dwellers on the earth, when an ensign is lifted up on the mountains, see ye ; and when the trumpet is blown, hear ye. For thus hath the Lord said unto me, I will be still, and I will behold in My dwelling-place ; like clear heat in sunshine, like a cloud of dew in the heat of harvest. For afore the harvest, when the blossom is over, and the flower becometh a ripening grape, He shall cut off the sprigs with pruning-hooks, and the spreading branches shall He take away and cut down. They shall be left together unto the ravenous birds of the mountains, and to the beasts of the earth : and the ravenous birds shall summer upon them, and all the beasts of the earth shall winter upon them. In that time shall a present be brought unto the Lord of hosts of a people tall and smooth, and from a people terrible from their beginning onward : a nation that meteth out and treadeth down, whose land the rivers divide, to the place of the name of the Lord of hosts, the Mount Zion.

At first Tirhakah's efforts were crowned with success. The ambassadors of Hezekiah made their way to Zoan and Hanes, or Herakleopolis, the two capitals of Egypt at the time (Is. xxx. 4), and from thence their presents to the Pharaoh were sent on the backs of camels through the desert of the south to the ancestral seat of Tirhakah in Ethiopia. It was not long before the Jewish envoys themselves followed 'in vessels of bulrushes,' pursuing the Ethiopian Pharaoh to his own southern land, 'which the rivers divide' (Is. xviii. 2), in the vain hope of obtaining help from 'a people that should not profit them.'

Meanwhile in Palestine itself a confederacy was organised. Hezekiah once more asserted his rights as a suzerain over the cities of the Philistines; the Assyrian satrap of Ashkelon was displaced in favour of a certain Zedekiah, whose name seems to indicate his Jewish origin; and Padi, of Ekron, who alone refused to break his oath of allegiance to Assyria, was carried to Jerusalem, and there thrown into chains. The Phœnician towns joined in the revolt against Assyrian authority, and the kings of Ammon, Moab, and Edom promised their aid. Tirhakah collected an army, and stationed himself on the Egyptian frontier, ready to move into Palestine when occasion required.

Sennacherib waited nearly three years before he considered himself sufficiently prepared to march towards the West. In B.C. 701 the great invasion took place. The Assyrian army was led by able generals, trained under Sargon, the father and predecessor of Sennacherib, and it proved too large to be resisted in the field by the allies. The Phœnician cities were captured before assistance could be brought to them, and the kings of Ammon, Moab, and Edom judged it prudent to make their peace with the conqueror. The Philistine towns were taken by storm, the south of Judah was devastated, and Hezekiah was forced to humble himself before the terrible invader, and to sue for pardon by the surrender of Padi, the payment of his former tribute, and the offer of numerous gifts. But Sennacherib was inexorable. Nothing would suffice him but the capitulation of Jerusalem, which would have placed Egypt at his mercy. Tirhakah was well awake to the danger which threatened himself, and his army had already left Egypt, and had reached Eltekeh, in the southern part of Judah.

The Assyrian forces were now divided into two, one portion being sent to besiege Jerusalem, while the rest endeavoured to check the advance of the Egyptians.

Nothing can show more clearly how large must have been the army employed by Sennacherib in the campaign, and how great a confidence must have been placed by the Assyrian leaders in their superiority in numbers. That confidence does not seem to have been misplaced, if we can trust the assertions of Sennacherib. He claims to have defeated the Egyptian army at Eltekeh, capturing in the battle the Ethiopian captains and ' the sons of the king of Egypt.' But it may be questioned whether his success was as complete as he represents it to have been. At all events, he did not follow up his victory, and contented himself with taking the little fortified villages of Eltekeh and Timnath. Tirhakah, on the other hand, was sufficiently weakened by the battle to be obliged to retreat, and to leave his ally Hezekiah to fall, as seemed inevitable, into the hands of his foe.

It was at this moment, when all human aid had been withdrawn, and the walls of Jerusalem alone stood between the Jewish king and his enemies, that the great disaster befell the triumphant Assyrian which is recorded in the pages of the Bible. God declared through the mouth of Isaiah that He would defend the city and line of David, ' for out of Jerusalem shall go forth a remnant, and they that escape out of Mount Zion [1].' The God of Israel was mightier than the Assyrian tyrant or the princes he had claimed to have overthrown. Sennacherib had boasted of his victory over the Egyptian monarch ; ' with the sole of his feet,' he had declared, he had ' dried

[1] Is. xxxvii. 32.

up all the arms of the Nile of Matsor[1].' But though Tirhakah had been thus driven back, leaving his ally Hezekiah to his fate, the divine aid was promised to the Jewish king, not for his own sake indeed, for Hezekiah had trusted to the arm of flesh and the bruised reed of Egypt, but for the sake of the Lord Himself and His servant David. So 'the angel of the Lord went forth and smote in the camp of the Assyrians a hundred and fourscore and five thousand.' The besieging army was annihilated, and the Assyrian king, who seems to have remained in the south on guard against a possible return of Tirhakah, hastily gathered his forces and his booty together and returned homewards to Nineveh. Like Xerxes after his defeat by the Greeks, Sennacherib never ventured again into the land where he had met with so signal an overthrow. As long as he lived Jerusalem was unmolested on the side of the Assyrians.

The deliverance from the invader was claimed by the Egyptians for the piety of their own king. The guides who showed Herodotus the antiquities of Memphis told him that when Sennacherib, 'the king of the Arabians and Assyrians,' attacked the country, it was governed, not by a monarch of the royal line, but by a priest of Ptah named Sethos, who deprived the military class of the lands assigned to them by former kings. Accordingly they refused to fight against the enemy, and left him to oppose Sennacherib as best he could with an army of artisans and tradesmen. Then Sethos entered the house of his god, and wept and prayed before the image, until a deep sleep fell upon him, during which

[1] Is. xxxvii. 25. The Authorised Version renders the Hebrew less accurately, 'the rivers of the besieged places.' Matsor denoted Northern Egypt, Pathros (Is. xi. 11) being Southern Egypt, and the two together forming Mizraim or the 'two Matsors.'

Ptah revealed himself to the sleeper and promised him victory over the foe. The promise was speedily fulfilled. While the Assyrian host was still encamped at Pelusion, on the frontiers of Egypt, an army of mice entered their camp as they slept and gnawed through their bowstrings, so that they fell an easy prey on the morrow to the followers of the Egyptian king.

The legend has plainly been modelled on the history recorded in the Bible, even the priestly character of Sethos being based on the religious reforms of Hezekiah ; and Egyptian vanity has flattered itself not only by claiming the credit of overthrowing the Assyrians, but also by ignoring the fact that Egypt in the time of Sennacherib's campaign was governed by an Ethiopian conqueror. It is needless to say that authentic history knows nothing of Sethos, while the story of the mice was suggested to the guides of Herodotus by the figure of a mouse in the hands of a god whose image he was shown at Memphis.

Whether Tirhakah made an effort to recover the ancient influence of Egypt in Palestine, after the retreat of Sennacherib, we do not know. At all events, there seems to be no reference to anything of the kind in the prophecies of Isaiah or Micah. It is probable that the defeat he had suffered at Eltekeh had weakened his power too greatly to allow him much opportunity for doing anything else than confirm his own authority in Egypt. Hezekiah died five years after the Assyrian overthrow (B. C. 696), and the accession of his son Man- asseh at the early age of twelve brought with it all the evils of a minority, which were further increased by his relapse into idolatry. The friends and councillors who had surrounded his father were removed or put to death, for 'Manasseh shed innocent blood very much, till he had filled Jerusalem from one end to another.' The persecution was especially severe against the prophets who denounced his idolatries and the profanation of the temple of the Lord. It is therefore possible that the internal troubles of Judah and the loss of the *prestige* which had surrounded the name of Hezekiah may have tempted Tirhakah to establish his influence in Jerusalem. None of the prophets who lived in the earlier part of Manasseh's reign have left us any remains; Isaiah, Micah and Hosea all alike ended their public ministry during the reign of Hezekiah. No light, consequently, is thrown upon the question by the Jewish records. It is true that on a statue in the Bulak Museum Tirhakah claims to have conquered the Khita or Syrians as well as the people of Arvad; but the scribe may here have merely been repeating the language used of an earlier king. All that we know with certainty is that Manasseh was a tributary vassal of Esar-haddon, who succeeded his father Sennacherib in B.C. 681, and that accordingly the independence of Judah from the Assyrian yoke so successfully achieved by Hezekiah was of no long duration.

The first result of the renewal of Assyrian authority and influence in Judah was the invasion of Egypt by the Assyrian king. This time the attack was successful. Tirhakah had persuaded Baal of Tyre to revolt against Esar-haddon, and to place the Phœnician fleet at his own disposal. But Esar-haddon blockaded Tyre with a portion of his forces, while with the remainder he marched southward towards the frontiers of Egypt. He met with no resistance on the way, and his army was supplied with water in its march through the desert by a Bedouin chief. Tirhakah was defeated in a pitched battle, and fled to Thebes, leaving Memphis, with his wives and concubines, his officers and treasure, at the mercy of Esar-haddon. The Assyrian monarch divided the country into twenty satrapies, placing the majority of them under native princes, but filling certain posts with Assyrian garrisons.

Tirhakah did not long remain quiet. In B.C. 669 Esarhaddon died, and his son and successor Assur-bani-pal found himself called upon to quell an Egyptian revolt. Tirhakah had returned to the north, and had entered Memphis in triumph, driving the Assyrian garrison before him. But his triumph was short-lived. The approach of the Assyrian army compelled him once more to retreat, and on this occasion he did not find a place of refuge until he had reached the Ethiopian capital Napata. He continued, however, to intrigue with the Egyptian princes, and before long Egypt was again handed over to war and confusion. Sais and other towns which had headed the outbreak were taken by storm, and their leaders sent in chains to Nineveh. Tirhakah, who had advanced to Memphis, was driven back to the Soudân, where he died shortly afterwards, after a reign of twenty-six years. His successor was Rut-Amun, the son of Sabako, who resumed the war against the Assyrians. Thebes opened its gates to him, and the Assyrian garrison was expelled from Memphis. But an Assyrian army soon entered Egypt, and the Egyptian soldiers fled before their terrible antagonists. The petty kings who had taken part in the insurrection were punished, and the Assyrian forces sailed up the river to Thebes, where a fearful vengeance was inflicted on the unfortunate city. Its temples and palaces were destroyed, its innumerable treasures carried off, and two

obelisks, seventy tons in weight, sent as trophies to
Nineveh. Thebes never recovered from the blow. The
ruin of its mighty temples mostly dates from its overthrow by the Assyrians, and the former capital of
Egypt sank gradually into the condition of a small
village. It is little wonder that Nahum (iii. 8), writing
while the news of the event was still ringing in the ears
of the neighbouring nations, should have asked whether
Nineveh were ' better than No of Amun[1],' so that it
should be spared the destruction it had brought upon
the Egyptian city. ' Ethiopia and Egypt were her
strength, and it was infinite : the men of Somali (Punt)
and of Libya were thy helpers. Yet was she carried
away, she went into captivity[2].' When Egypt recovered
her independence under Psammetikhos (B.C. 660), and
shook off for ever the Assyrian yoke, it was no longer in
Thebes, but in the cities of the north, that the seat of the
renovated empire was fixed.

Isaiah had foreseen in prophetic vision the disasters that
were to come upon the Egyptians. The Rab-shakeh[3]
of Assyria had warned the Jews against trusting to the
staff of its broken reed, but Isaiah had described in plain
language (ch. xix.) the troubles which Egypt was so
speedily to experience. We again quote his words :—

The burden of Egypt.
Behold, the Lord rideth upon a swift cloud, and cometh unto
Egypt: and the idols of Egypt shall be moved at His presence, and
the heart of Egypt shall melt in the midst of it. And I will stir up
the Egyptians against the Egyptians: and they shall fight every
one against his brother, and every on against his neighbour;

[1] Mistranslated ' populous No' in the Authorised Version.
[2] Nahum iii. 9.
[3] In Assyrian, Rab-saki, ' chief of the princes,' a title of the Vizier or
Prime Minister.

city against city, and kingdom against kingdom. And the spirit of
Egypt shall be made void in the midst of it ; and I will destroy the
counsel thereof : and they shall seek unto the idols, and to the
charmers, and to them that have familiar spirits, and to the wizards.
And I will give over the Egyptians into the hand of a cruel lord ;
and a fierce king shall rule over them, saith the Lord, the Lord of
hosts. And the waters shall fail from the sea, and the river shall
be wasted and become dry. And the rivers shall stink ; the
streams of Egypt shall be minished and dried up : the reeds and
flags shall wither away. The meadows by the Nile, by the brink
of the Nile, and all that is sown by the Nile, shall become dry, be
driven away, and be no more. The fishers also shall lament, and
all they that cast angle into the Nile shall mourn, and they that
spread nets upon the waters shall languish. Moreover they that
work in combed flax, and they that weave white cloth, shall be
ashamed. And her pillars shall be broken in pieces, all they that
work for hire shall be grieved in soul. The princes of Zoan are
utterly foolish : the counsel of the wisest counsellors of Pharaoh is
become brutish : how say ye unto Pharaoh, I am the son of the
wise, the son of ancient kings? Where then are thy wise men?
and let them tell thee now ; and let them know what the Lord
of hosts hath purposed concerning Egypt. The princes of Zoan
are become fools, the princes of Noph are deceived : they have
caused Egypt to go astray, that are the corner-stone of her tribes.
The Lord hath mingled a spirit of perverseness in the midst of her :
and they have caused Egypt to go astray in every work thereof, as
a drunken man staggereth in his vomit. Neither shall there be
for Egypt any work, which head or tail, palm-branch or rush,
may do.

In that day shall Egypt be like unto women : and it shall tremble
and fear because of the shaking of the hand of the Lord of hosts,
which He shaketh over it. And the land of Judah shall become a
terror unto Egypt, every one to whom mention is made thereof
shall be afraid, because of the purpose of the Lord of hosts, which
He purposeth against it.

In that day there shall be five cities in the land of Egypt that
speak the language of Canaan, and swear to the Lord of hosts ; one
shall be called The city of destruction.

In that day shall there be an altar to the Lord in the midst of

the land of Egypt, and a pillar at the border thereof to the Lord.
And it shall be for a sign and for a witness unto the Lord of hosts
in the land of Egypt: for they shall cry unto the Lord because of
the oppressors, and He shall send them a saviour, and a defender,
and he shall deliver them. And the Lord shall be known to Egypt,
and the Egyptians shall know the Lord in that day; yea, they
shall worship with sacrifice and oblation, and shall vow a vow unto
the Lord, and shall perform it. And the Lord shall smite Egypt,
smiting and healing; and they shall return unto the Lord, and He
shall be intreated of them, and shall heal them.

In that day shall there be a high way out of Egypt to Assyria,
and the Assyrian shall come into Egypt, and the Egyptian into
Assyria: and the Egyptians shall worship with the Assyrians.

In that day shall Israel be the third with Egypt and with
Assyria, a blessing in the midst of the earth: for that the Lord of
hosts hath blessed them, saying, Blessed be Egypt My people, and
Assyria the work of My hands, and Israel Mine inheritance.

The land of Judah was thus to be a terror unto Egypt;
for it was out of Judah that the destroying hosts of
Assyria were to march, secure of the submission of the
vassal king of Jerusalem. So far from being able to
afford assistance to Judah, Egypt was to regard Judah
as a formidable neighbour. The Jewish party, therefore, which sought for an alliance with Egypt, was
pursuing a policy which on human as well as on divine
grounds was utterly fatal. The party was in high favour
in the time of Hezekiah; it seemed to advocate the
only line of policy by which the independence of the
Jewish state could be secured, and Isaiah's opposition
and words of warning were disregarded.

But events showed that he was right. The alliance
with Egypt, which had been purchased with the treasures
of Jerusalem, and the toilsome journey of the Jewish
ambassadors into the heart of Ethiopia, was shattered by
the battle of Eltekeh, while the overthrow of the army of

Sennacherib before Jerusalem proved that trust in their God was the only defence the rulers of Judah needed, and that their strength was, as Isaiah had declared, 'to sit still[1].' From that time onwards, to the death of Hezekiah, there was no more straining after an Egyptian alliance, and Isaiah's later years were cheered by the consciousness that the policy he had preached and struggled for was at last triumphant. For nearly a century Egypt disappeared from the political horizon of the Jews.

[1] Is. xxx. 7. This is the rendering of the Authorised Version, and is in harmony with verse 15: 'In returning and rest shall ye be saved; in quietness and in confidence shall be your strength: and ye would not.' Most modern scholars, however, prefer to refer the words of verse 7 to Egypt, translating 'therefore have I cried concerning her (i.e. Egypt), She is arrogant (and) slothful.'

CHAPTER III.

ASSYRIA.

WHEN Isaiah was born the name of Assyria excited no feelings of terror or apprehension in the mind of the Jew. It was remembered that an Assyrian king had once marched his armies to the west, and exacted tribute not only from the cities of Phœnicia, but also from Jehu of Israel, and that at a later period (B.C. 804) another Assyrian king had taken the city of Damascus by storm : but such events had left no lasting impression upon the political map of Palestine, and no Assyrian army had approached the frontier of the kingdom of Judah itself. All that was known in the west about Assyria was that it was in a decaying condition. The old dynasty of kings had lost its military character, and the Assyrian troops had a hard struggle to maintain the northern boundaries of the kingdom against the attacks of Ararat or Van. But in B.C. 745 an event happened which had a profound effect on the course of history in Western Asia. The last monarch of the old line died or was put to death, and the throne was seized by a military adventurer called Pulu or Pul, who took the name of Tiglath-pileser III.

This Tiglath-pileser was a man of great ability and force of character. He excelled as a commander ; he equally excelled as an administrator and civil organiser. Under him the Assyrian army became once more the scourge of the surrounding nations ; nothing could resist it ; and the leagues which were formed against the

advance of Assyrian ambition were scattered like
stubble in the wind. Victory after victory attended
upon the new Assyrian king and his generals. But
his campaigns were not mere raids for the sake of
plunder, like those of earlier Assyrian sovereigns; they
were all conceived with a definite object and carried
out according to a definite plan. Tiglath-pileser
determined to found an empire in Western Asia which
should embrace the whole of the civilised world, and the
centre of which should be Nineveh. It was a new idea in
history. Hitherto a royal conqueror had been content with
exacting tribute, which was paid by the conquered people
as long as the foreign army was near them, and refused
as soon as it was withdrawn. The conquered districts
had to be reconquered again and again; they were never
welded into one with the conquering power and formed
into a homogeneous empire. To found such an empire
was the task undertaken by Tiglath-pileser. Slowly,
but surely, he extended the Assyrian sway, turning the
conquered countries into Assyrian provinces under
Assyrian satraps appointed by the supreme king himself.
The taxes to be paid by the newly-constituted satrapies
were carefully apportioned, and a great civil bureaucracy
was organised, which had its centre and head in Nineveh.
For the first time in the history of the world the conception of imperial centralisation was formed, and an
attempt was made to realise it in fact.

The second Assyrian empire, founded by Tiglath-
pileser, was thus a new experiment in political history.
It marks the beginning of a new era. Based upon
military aggression, it was consolidated and carried on
by civil law. There was to be one law and government
throughout the world, one supreme monarch to obey,

one supreme deity—Assur, the national god of Assyria—
to revere.

Isaiah was not very old before Judah had reason
to know that a new and terrible power had arisen
on the banks of the Tigris. In B.C. 742 the first contact
took place between Judah and Assyria. The contact
was a hostile one. Tiglath-pileser threatened Hamath,
which had found an ally in Azariah of Jerusalem. From
the time of David onwards there had always been
friendly relations between Hamath and Judah. They
each had a common enemy in the intervening power of
Syria. The overthrow of the Syrian prince Hadadezer
had brought about an alliance between Tou of Hamath
and the Jewish conqueror, and when the kingdom of
Damascus was established on the ruins of David's
empire we may gather from 2 Kings xiv. 28 that in
the days of Jeroboam II a peculiar bond of union still
continued to exist between Hamath and Judah. The
same fact appears very clearly on the Assyrian monuments. The people of Hamath, as we learn from them,
were supported in their resistance to Assyria by Azariah,
the Jewish king, and accordingly nineteen districts of
Hamath, 'which in their wickedness had plotted with
Azariah,' were overrun by the Assyrian troops and
placed under an Assyrian governor.

So long, however, as the rich and powerful kingdom
of the Hittites lasted, with its capital Carchemish com-
manding the fords of the Euphrates and the high-road
to the West, it was impossible for the Assyrian monarch
to establish his authority firmly in Syria and Palestine.
But Carchemish had been weakened by the intestine
divisions of the Hittite states, as well as by attacks from
without, and, in spite of the assistance brought to it by

the wilder Hittite tribes of the northern mountains, the day of its final overthrow was near. Tiglath-pileser was able to neglect it for the present, and to concentrate his attention on the affairs of Damascus and Phœnicia.

In B.C. 738 we find him receiving tribute from Menahem of Samaria, Rezon of Damascus, and Hiram of Tyre. The payment of tribute implied the admission of the paramount authority of the Assyrian king, and proved that by this time the Syrian princes were fully awake to the dangers which threatened them on the side of Assyria. They soon afforded another proof of their anxiety on this score. The throne of Israel was occupied at the time by Pekah, a successful general who had murdered his predecessor, but who was evidently a man of vigour and ability. He and Rezon endeavoured to form a confederacy of the Syrian and Palestinian states against their common Assyrian foe. In order to effect their object they considered it necessary to displace the reigning king of Judah, Ahaz, and substitute for him a creature of their own. The latter is called ' the son of Tabeel' (Is. vii. 6), a name which seems to be of Syrian origin, and consequently to indicate that the bearer of it was a Syrian by birth. But the people of Judah rallied round the house of David, in spite of the weak and unworthy character of its representative, and the allies were compelled to resort to arms in order to impose their nominee upon Jerusalem. They were aided by a party of malcontents in Judah itself (Is. viii. 6), and the position of Ahaz seemed desperate. His forces had been beaten in the field, the Syrian army had made its way to the extreme south of the country, and had even wrested from Judah its naval port of Elath, on the Gulf of Akabah, while the Philistines had taken advantage of the occasion to invade and annex the neighbouring Jewish towns[1]. In this moment of peril Isaiah was instructed to meet and comfort Ahaz. He bade him 'fear not, neither be faint-hearted,' for the confederacy against the dynasty of David should be broken and overthrown. All that Ahaz was called upon to do was to 'be quiet,' to adopt a policy of patient expectancy; awaiting the time when Damascus and Samaria should alike be destroyed by that Assyrian power which they were vainly essaying to stem. But Ahaz had already determined on the policy he intended to pursue. He had no faith either in the prophet or in the message he was commissioned to deliver. He saw safety in one course only—that of invoking the assistance of the Assyrian king, and bribing him by the offer of homage and tribute to march against his enemies.

In vain Isaiah denounced so suicidal and unpatriotic a policy. In vain he foretold that when Damascus and Samaria had been crushed, the next victim of the Assyrian king would be Judah itself. The infatuated Ahaz would not listen. He 'sent messengers to Tiglath-pileser king of Assyria, saying, I am thy servant and thy son: come up, and save me out of the hand of the king of Syria, and out of the hand of the king of Israel, which rise up against me[2].'

Tiglath-pileser was ready enough to obey. He had been looking for an opportunity to interfere in the West, and this was afforded by the Jewish king. He could now march his armies past the Hittite fortress of Car-chemish, and proceed leisurely to the conquest of Syria, secure in the knowledge that the equally important

---

[1] See 2 Kings xvi. 6; 2 Chron. xxviii. 17, 18.
[2] Compare Is. vii. with 2 Kings xvi. 7.

fortress of Jerusalem was upon his side, preventing the Egyptians from moving to the help of the Syrian prince. Ahaz thus enabled Tiglath-pileser to effect with comparatively little difficulty what might otherwise have been a slow and arduous work. At the same time, by voluntarily acknowledging himself the vassal of Assyria, he laid a lasting yoke upon his country and successors, and made all future attempts at independence rebellions against their liege lord.

In the fragmentary annals of Tiglath-pileser, Ahaz is called Jehoahaz, a name which signifies 'the Lord has laid hold.' It is evident, therefore, that the sacred historians have deprived the name of the Jewish king of the divine element (Jeho) which they considered him to have profaned.

His tribute was paid in B.C. 734. The Assyrian king must already have been in the West. He lost little time, therefore, in hurling his forces upon the confederate powers of Damascus and Samaria. Rezon was overthrown in a decisive battle, his chariots destroyed, his captains captured and impaled, and himself compelled to fly for refuge to his capital, Damascus. Here he was closely besieged by a portion of the Assyrian army, the beautiful gardens by which the city was surrounded being despoiled of their trees for use in the siege. Tiglath-pileser with the rest of his troops carried fire and sword through the sixteen districts of Syria, and then proceeded to fall upon Samaria. The northern part of the country was overrun, and the tribes on the eastern side of the Jordan carried into captivity. Gilead and Abel-beth-Maachath are among the places mentioned by name in the Assyrian annals as having been sacked, in accordance with the statement of 2 Kings

xv. 29. The Assyrian monarch now pursued his victorious march to the south. Ammon and Moab, which had aided Israel and Syria in their assault upon Judah, were compelled to submit, and troops were sent against Edom and the queen of the Arabs, who had also taken part in the war against Ahaz (see 2 Chron. xxviii. 17, 18). Tiglath-pileser next turned westward towards the sea-coast, in order to punish the Philistines. Their old hostility to the Jewish monarchy had doubtless led them to support Rezon, the weakness of Judah affording them an opportunity of throwing off the Jewish yoke. They had found a leader in Khanun or Hanno of Gaza, who escaped into Egypt upon the approach of the Assyrian army, leaving his city to the mercy of the enemy. Tiglath-pileser contented himself with laying it under tribute, carrying away its gods, and erecting an image of himself in the temple of Dagon. Ekron and Ashdod were punished at the same time, and Metinti of Ashkelon committed suicide, in order to escape the vengeance of the conqueror. As Gath is not mentioned, it would appear that it had already disappeared from history.

From the cities of Philistia Tiglath-pileser made his way into the territory of Israel. Pekah was now left destitute of allies, and face to face with the irresistible conqueror. Samaria soon fell into the hands of the Assyrians, and Pekah was put to death. According to Tiglath-pileser, the execution was by his order, Hoshea being appointed in his place as a tributary vassal of Assyria. The Old Testament informs us that the instrument for carrying out the commands of the Assyrian king was Hoshea, the son of Elah, himself (2 Kings xv. 30).

Meanwhile Damascus had at last surrendered, after a siege of two years (B.C. 732). Rezon was slain, his subjects transported to Kir (2 Kings xvi. 9), and the neighbouring princes summoned to his palace, there to do homage to the Assyrian king. Among those who came was Ahaz of Judah, in company with Sanib of Ammon, Solomon or Shalman of Moab, Kavus-melech of Edom, and Hanno of Gaza, who had succeeded in bringing about a reconciliation between himself and 'the great king.'

It was while he was at Damascus that Ahaz saw the altar of which he sent a pattern to Urijah the priest at Jerusalem. It had doubtless been dedicated to Rimmon, the sun-god of Syria, and it was this altar of a heathen and vanquished deity that Ahaz, fascinated perhaps by its size, now determined to substitute for the brazen altar in the temple of the Lord. Before his return to Jerusalem the subservient priest had carried out his instructions. The new altar was set up in front of the sanctuary, and the older one transferred to its northern side. Ahaz offered upon it solemn sacrifice, in commemoration of his return in 'peace,' and enjoined Urijah henceforward to burn upon it 'the morning burnt offering, and the evening meat offering, and the king's burnt sacrifice, and his meat offering, with the burnt offering of all the people of the land, and their meat offering and their drink offerings;' while the brazen altar was reserved for the purposes of an oracle, where Ahaz might 'enquire' the will of Heaven (2 Kings xvi. 10–16).

This Syrian altar, however, was not the only fruit of the visit of Ahaz to Damascus. We hear in Isa. xxxviii. 8 of the 'sun-dial of Ahaz,' and it is difficult

not to see in this a proof of Assyrian influence. The
Babylonians were celebrated throughout the ancient
world for their astronomical lore, and the invention of the
gnomon or sun-dial is ascribed to them. In astronomy,
as in other branches of learning, the Assyrians were
the pupils of the Babylonians, and through the Assyrians the form and use of the sun-dial might easily
have become known to the Jewish king. It is possible
that the library of Jerusalem, where, as we learn from
Prov. xxv. 1, scribes were employed in copying and
editing ancient works, like the scribes of the Assyrian
and Babylonian libraries, was also founded by Ahaz.
At all events, it seems to have owed its origin to that
contact with Assyria for which Ahaz was first respon-
sible, and which led in some measure to the outburst
of literary activity that marked the age of Isaiah.

For nearly six years Hoshea remained faithful to
Assyria. But in B.C. 727 Tiglath-pileser died, and
the throne was seized by a general of the army, who
took the name of Shalmaneser IV. The second Assyrian empire had been founded upon usurpation and
military force, and what its founder had successfully
achieved other generals thought they might achieve too.
The moment seemed a favourable one to Hoshea to
renounce his allegiance to the Assyrians. In earlier
times a distant conquest had been retained by them
only so long as the conqueror lived or had energy and
power enough to punish any attempt at disaffection.
The conquests of the older Assyrian kings had been
raids rather than permanent annexations of territory.
Hoshea doubtless imagined that the conquests of Tiglath-
pileser, like those of his predecessors, would melt away
as soon as the strong hand that had effected them was

removed. But he was soon undeceived. It was an empire in the true sense of the word that Tiglath-pileser had succeeded in establishing, and the empire was maintained by a standing army of veteran soldiers, commanded by able generals who shared the views and policy of Tiglath-pileser himself. A change of sovereigns accordingly made little difference in the policy of Assyria. It was carried on by men all trained in the same military and political school, and bent on carrying out to their accomplishment the designs of their master. Hoshea's attempt at rebellion was promptly crushed. Unable to find allies elsewhere, he had turned to Sabako of Egypt, and, like Hezekiah in later days, had found the Ethiopian but a bruised reed. Before Sabako could move to his assistance, Hoshea was defeated by the Assyrian king or his satraps, and thrown into chains. The ruling classes of Samaria, however, still held out. An Assyrian army, accordingly, once more devastated the land of Israel, and laid siege to its capital.

For three years Samaria remained untaken. Another revolution had meanwhile broken out in Assyria; Shalmaneser had died or been put to death, and a fresh military adventurer had seized the crown, taking the name of Sargon, after a famous monarch of ancient Babylonia. Sargon had hardly established himself upon the throne when Samaria fell (B.C. 722). The spoil he carried away from it shows pretty plainly the condition in which Hoshea had left his kingdom. Ahab had once been able to send 2000 chariots to the help of Hadadezer in his struggle against Assyria; now Sargon found no more than fifty in the Israelitish capital. He contented himself with transporting only 27,280 of its inhabitants

D

into captivity, only the upper classes in fact, who were implicated in the revolt of Hoshea. An Assyrian satrap, or governor, was appointed over Samaria, while the bulk of the population was allowed to remain peaceably in their old homes[1].

Sargon was a rough but able soldier, and under him the Assyrian army became irresistible. His reign witnessed the consolidation of the empire and the fulfilment for the most part of Tiglath-pileser's designs. The main objects of his policy and military campaigns were twofold. On the one side he aimed at turning the whole of Western Asia into an integral part of the Assyrian dominion, and thus diverting the maritime trade of Phœnicia and the inland trade of the Hittites into Assyrian hands. On the other side, he desired to consecrate and legitimise his power by the possession of Babylonia. Babylonia was the cradle of Assyrian culture and religion; it was the sacred motherland from which Asshur had gone forth in prehistoric days to build the cities of Assyria. The Assyrian regarded it as the mediæval German regarded Rome; to be crowned king at Babylon gave the Assyrian monarch the same title to veneration that coronation at Rome gave to a Charlemagne or an Otho. It was the visible sign of sovereignty in the valleys of the Tigris and Euphrates, a proof that Bel had set apart the sovereign as the rightful successor of the heroes and princes of old. What the kings of the second Assyrian empire wanted in legitimacy of birth, they sought to obtain by the conquest of Babylon.

Tiglath-pileser had made himself master of Babylonia immediately after his conquest of Damascus, and a year

---

[1] This is in accordance with 2 Chron. xxx, xxxi.

or two before his death had 'taken the hand of Bel,' a ceremony which announced to the world that the chief god of Babylon had accepted him as the lawful defender of the city. In Babylonia he retained his original name of Pul, since that of Tiglath-pileser belonged to a former king of Assyria whose relations with Babylonia had been the reverse of friendly. Sargon, on the other hand, assumed a name which marked him out as specially a Babylonian, and in virtue of it claimed from the outset of his reign the sovereignty of Babylon. For the present, however, the claim could be asserted only, not made good. Babylonia had been occupied by Merodach-baladan, 'the son of Yagina,' and chief of a Chaldean tribe settled in the marshes at the mouth of the Euphrates, who for twelve years succeeded in keeping the Assyrian king at bay. Sargon meanwhile was busily employed in strengthening his northern and eastern frontiers against the wild tribes of Kurdistan, and in completing the subjugation of Western Asia.

Two years after the fall of Samaria (B.C. 720) he had again been summoned to the West. Hamath had broken into revolt, and induced Damascus, Arpad, and Samaria to follow her example. Promises of aid had been received from Egypt, while the restless Khanun of Gaza had again declared himself independent of Assyria. It is possible that Hezekiah, who had now succeeded his father Ahaz, may also have been concerned in the movement. At all events, the name of the Hamathite king Yahu-bihdi, which is once written El-bihdi, contains the name of the God of Israel, and the friendship between Hamath and Judah was, as we have seen, of long standing.

However this may be, the rebels proved no match for

the Assyrian king. Yahu-bihdi was captured at Aroer,
and flayed alive; Hamath was colonised by Assyrians
under an Assyrian governor, while its former inhabitants
were transplanted to Samaria. The Assyrian army then
marched southward ; the Egyptian forces were routed at
Raphia, and Khanun fell into the hands of his enemies.
For nine years Palestine remained sullenly submissive to
Assyrian rule.

The interval was used by Sargon in securing his road
to the Mediterranean. In B.C. 717, Carchemish, the rich
capital of the Hittites south of the Taurus, fell into his
hands, and along with it the command of the great ford
across the Euphrates, and the commerce which passed
over it. In vain the kinsfolk and allies of the people of
Carchemish came to their assistance from the moun-
tainous regions of the north. The shock of their attack
was broken by the trained valour of the Assyrian forces ;
Sargon carried the war into the wild regions of Asia
Minor, and Carchemish passed for ever out of Hittite
possession. Henceforward it became the seat of an
Assyrian satrap.

Assyria was now connected with its possessions in the
West by a well-guarded and continuous road. The hope
of successful resistance to its domination had become
wellnigh desperate. The tributary kingdoms which lay
south of the Assyrian satrapy of Samaria served only as
a thin screen of division between the decaying power of
Egypt and the ever-increasing and ever-menacing might
of Nineveh. The Assyrian had indeed come in like a
flood. In the south Merodach-baladan, backed by the
armies of Elam, still governed an independent Babylonia ;
but as year by year went by, and the power of Sargon
steadily grew and consolidated, he saw the doom that

awaited him nearing in the distance. It could not be
long before the Assyrian king would consider that all
was ripe for the invasion of Babylonia.

Merodach-baladan therefore determined to anticipate
the attack. In the neighbouring monarchy of Elam he
had a powerful, though untrustworthy ally ; but his only
chance of successfully resisting the invader was by forcing
him to divide his forces. If he could induce Egypt and
Palestine to rise in arms at the same time that he himself
fell upon Sargon from the south, there was a hope that
the common enemy could be crushed. and that the
terrible scourge which was afflicting all Western Asia
might be overthrown.

In the fourteenth year of Hezekiah's reign (B.C. 711),
accordingly, ambassadors came from the court of Babylon, under the pretext of congratulating the Jewish king
on his recovery from sickness. Their real object, however, was something very different. It was to concert
measures with Hezekiah for a general uprising in the
West, and for the formation of a league against Sargon,
which should embrace at once Babylonia, Palestine, and
Elam. Hezekiah was flattered by such a proof of his
own importance. He opened the gates of his armoury
and treasure-house, and showed the ambassadors the
accumulated stores of wealth and arms which he was
ready to lavish on the war. Isaiah thus describes his
weakness :—

At that time Merodach-baladan the son of Baladan, king of
Babylon, sent letters and a present to Hezekiah: for he heard that
he had been sick, and was recovered. And Hezekiah was glad of
them, and shewed them the house of his precious things, the silver,
and the gold, and the spices, and the precious oil, and all the house
of his armour, and all that was found in his treasures: there was

nothing in his house, nor in all his dominion, that Hezekiah shewed them not. Then came Isaiah the prophet unto king Hezekiah, and said unto him, What said these men? and from whence came they unto thee? And Hezekiah said, They are come from a far country unto me, even from Babylon. Then said he, What have they seen in thine house? And Hezekiah answered, All that is in mine house have they seen : there is nothing among my treasures that I have not shewed them. Then said Isaiah to Hezekiah, Hear the word of the Lord of hosts. Behold, the days come, that all that is in thine house, and that which thy fathers have laid up in store until this day, shall be carried to Babylon : nothing shall be left, saith the Lord. And of thy sons that shall issue from thee, which thou shalt beget, shall they take away; and they shall be eunuchs in the palace of the king of Babylon. Then said Hezekiah unto Isaiah, Good is the word of the Lord which thou hast spoken. He said moreover, For there shall be peace and truth in my days.

That policy of quietude, of ' sitting still,' which Isaiah had preached, was forgotten, and the Jewish king proved himself only too ready to ally himself with heathen powers, to break his plighted word to Assyria, and to rely for salvation on ' the arm of flesh.' When Isaiah came to him with stern rebuke and the prophecy that a day should come when his treasures should be carried indeed to Babylon, but in the train of a conqueror, Hezekiah bent his head in apparent contrition, but made no effort to withdraw himself from the political combination in which he had promised to be an actor.

Sargon, however, was not blind to what was going on. The pretext upon which the Babylonian ambassadors had sought the court of Hezekiah did not deceive him, and he resolved to strike before the enemy could unite their forces. Palestine was the first to suffer. Akhimit, whom the Assyrians had appointed king of Ashdod, had been dethroned, and a certain Yavan, ' the Greek,' had been put in his place, probably by Hezekiah. Ashdod thus became the centre of the opposition to Assyrian authority. Its punishment was not long delayed. Sargon swept 'the widespread land of Judah,' and coerced the Edomites and Moabites, while the Ethiopian king of Egypt hid himself behind the frontiers of the Delta. The Tartan or commander-in-chief was sent against Ashdod; the city was captured and razed to the ground, its inhabitants sold into slavery, and the unfortunate Yavan, who had escaped into Egypt, was handed over by his cowardly hosts to the mercy of his enemy [1].

Sargon himself seems at the time to have been in Judah. Though he has left us no details of the campaign, beyond the general statement that he overran 'the broad fields of the Jews,' we may gather from the pages of Isaiah that he had invested the Jewish capital and compelled it to surrender to him. The prophecy contained in the 10th and 11th chapters of the prophet's book seems to have been uttered when the implacable Assyrian was already at Nob, within a day's journey only of Jerusalem. We reproduce the prophet's exact words, in order that the reader may the better appreciate the force of the argument here :—

Ho Assyrian, the rod of Mine anger, the staff in whose hand is Mine indignation! I will send him against a profane nation, and against the people of My wrath will I give him a charge, to take the spoil, and to take the prey, and to tread them down like the mire of the streets. Howbeit he meaneth not so, neither doth his heart think so; but it is in his heart to destroy, and to cut off nations not a few. For he saith, Are not my princes all of them kings? Is not Calno as Carchemish? is not Hamath as Arpad? is not Samaria as Damascus? As my hand hath found the kingdoms of the idols, whose graven images did excel them of Jerusalem and of Samaria;

---

[1] See Is. xx. 1.

shall I not, as I have done unto Samaria and her idols, so do to Jerusalem and her idols?

Wherefore it shall come to pass, that when the Lord hath performed His whole work upon Mount Zion and on Jerusalem, I will punish the fruit of the stout heart of the king of Assyria, and the glory of his high looks. For he hath said, By the strength of my hand I have done it, and by my wisdom; for I am prudent: and I have removed the bounds of the peoples, and have robbed their treasures, and I have brought down as a valiant man them that sit on thrones: and my hand hath found as a nest the riches of the peoples; and as one gathereth eggs that are forsaken, have I gathered all the earth: and there was none that moved the wing, or that opened the mouth, or chirped. Shall the axe boast itself against him that heweth therewith? shall the saw magnify itself against him that shaketh it? as if a rod should shake them that lift it up, or as if a staff should lift up him that is not wood.

Therefore shall the Lord, the Lord of hosts, send among his fat ones leanness; and under his glory there shall be kindled a burning like the burning of fire. And the light of Israel shall be for a fire, and his Holy One for a flame: and it shall burn and devour his thorns and his briers in one day. And he shall consume the glory of his forest, and of his fruitful field, both soul and body: and it shall be as when a standardbearer fainteth. And the remnant of the trees of his forest shall be few, that a child may write them.

And it shall come to pass in that day, that the remnant of Israel, and they that are escaped of the house of Jacob, shall no more again stay upon him that smote them; but shall stay upon the Lord, the Holy One of Israel, in truth. A remnant shall return, even the remnant of Jacob, unto the mighty God. For though thy people Israel be as the sand of the sea, only a remnant of them shall return: a consumption is determined, overflowing with righteousness. For a consummation, and that determined, shall the Lord, the Lord of hosts, make in the midst of all the earth.

Therefore thus saith the Lord, the Lord of hosts, O My people that dwellest in Zion, be not afraid of the Assyrian: though he smite thee with the rod, and lift up his staff against thee, after the manner of Egypt. For yet a very little while, and the indignation shall be accomplished, and Mine anger, in their destruction. And the Lord of hosts shall stir up against him a scourge, as in the slaughter of Midian at the rock of Oreb : and his rod shall be over the sea, and he shall lift it up after the manner of Egypt. And it shall come to pass in that day, that his burden shall depart from off thy shoulder, and his yoke from off thy neck, and the yoke shall be destroyed because of the anointing.

He is come to Aiath, he is passed through Migron : at Michmash he layeth up his baggage : they are gone over the pass ; they have taken up their lodging at Geba : Ramah trembleth ; Gibeah of Saul is fled. Cry aloud with thy voice, O daughter of Gallim! hearken, O Laishah! O thou poor Anathoth! Madmenah is a fugitive ; the inhabitants of Gebim gather themselves to flee. This very day shall he halt at Nob : he shaketh his hand at the mount of the daughter of Zion, the hill of Jerusalem.

Behold, the Lord, the Lord of hosts, shall lop the boughs with terror: and the high ones of stature shall be hewn down, and the lofty shall be brought low. And he shall cut down the thickets of the forest with iron, and Lebanon shall fall by a mighty one.

And there shall come forth a shoot out of the stock of Jesse, and a branch out of his roots shall bear fruit : and the Spirit of the Lord shall rest upon him, the spirit of wisdom and understanding, the spirit of counsel and might, the spirit of knowledge and of the fear of the Lord ; and his delight shall be in the fear of the Lord : and he shall not judge after the sight of his eyes, neither reprove after the hearing of his ears: but with righteousness shall he judge the poor, and reprove with equity for the meek of the earth : and he shall smite the earth with the rod of his mouth, and with the breath of his lips shall he slay the wicked. And righteousness shall be the girdle of his loins, and faithfulness the girdle of his reins. And the wolf shall dwell with the lamb, and the leopard shall lie down with the kid ; and the calf and the young lion and the fatling together ; and a little child shall lead them. And the cow and the bear shall feed ; their young ones shall lie down together: and the lion shall eat straw like the ox. And the sucking child shall play on the hole of the asp, and the weaned child shall put his hand on the basilisk's den. They shall not hurt nor destroy in all My holy mountain: for the earth shall be full of the knowledge of the Lord, as the waters cover the sea.

And it shall come to pass in that day, that the root of Jesse,

which standeth for an ensign of the peoples, unto him shall the
nations seek ; and his resting-place shall be glorious.

And it shall come to pass in that day, that the Lord shall set His
hand again the second time to recover the remnant of His people,
which shall remain, from Assyria, and from Egypt, and from Pathros, and from Cush, and from Elam, and from Shinar, and from
Hamath, and from the islands of the sea. And He shall set up an
ensign for the nations, and shall assemble the outcasts of Israel, and
gather together the dispersed of Judah from the four corners of the
earth. The envy also of Ephraim shall depart, and they that vex
Judah shall be cut off : Ephraim shall not envy Judah, and Judah
shall not vex Ephraim. And they shall fly down upon the shoulder
of the Philistines on the west ; together shall they spoil the children
of the east : they shall put forth their hand upon Edom and Moab ;
and the children of Ammon shall obey them. And the Lord shall
utterly destroy the tongue of the Egyptian sea ; and with his
scorching wind shall He shake His hand over the River, and shall
smite it into seven streams, and cause men to march over dryshod.
And there shall be an high way for the remnant of His people,
which shall remain, from Assyria ; like as there was for Israel in
the day that he came out of the land of Egypt.

Now this description cannot well apply to the later
Assyrian advance upon Jerusalem in the time of Sennacherib ; this was made from the south-west, from the
direction of Lachish and Libnah, not from the north-east,
along the high road which led from Syria and Samaria,
and conducted an invading army past Michmash and
Ramah, Anathoth and Nob. Moreover the tone adopted
by Isaiah is very different from that of the prophecy he
was commissioned to deliver when the hosts of Sennacherib were threatening the sacred city. Then Hezekiah and his people were encouraged by the promise
that the enemy should be utterly overthrown ; now, on
the contrary, the prophet declares that the Assyrian is
the rod of God's anger, and that though a remnant shall
return, and the oppressor be punished, it shall be only

when the measure of God's chastisement of His people is complete, when they have been trodden down like mire in the streets, and when the high ones of stature have been hewn down. The contents of the prophecy also point unmistakeably to the age of Sargon. The Assyrian king is made to boast of his conquests of Carchemish and Hamath, of Arpad, Damascus and Samaria, all of them achievements of Sargon, not of his son Sennacherib.

The 'burden' contained in the 22nd chapter would also seem to belong to the age of Sargon. Again we reproduce Isaiah's words :—

The burden of the valley of vision.

What aileth thee now, that thou art wholly gone up to the housetops? O thou that art full of shoutings, a tumultuous city, a joyous town; thy slain are not slain with the sword, neither are they dead in battle. All thy rulers fled away together, they were bound by the archers: all that were found of thee were bound together, they fled afar off. Therefore said I, Look away from me, I will weep bitterly; labour not to comfort me, for the spoiling of the daughter of my people. For it is a day of discomfiture, and of treading down, and of perplexity, from the Lord, the Lord of hosts, in the valley of vision; a breaking down of the walls, and a crying to the mountains. And Elam bare the quiver, with chariots of men and horsemen; and Kir uncovered the shield. And it came to pass, that thy choicest valleys were full of chariots, and the horsemen set themselves in array at the gate. And he took away the covering of Judah; and thou didst look in that day to the armour in the house of the forest. And ye saw the breaches of the city of David, that they were many: and ye gathered together the waters of the lower pool. And ye numbered the houses of Jerusalem, and ye brake down the houses to fortify the wall. Ye made also a reservoir between the two walls for the water of the old pool: but ye looked not unto him that had done this, neither had ye respect unto him that fashioned it long ago. And in that day did the Lord, the Lord of hosts, call to weeping, and to mourning, and to baldness, and to girding with sackcloth: and behold, joy and gladness, slaying oxen and killing sheep, eating flesh and drinking wine: let us eat and drink, for to-morrow we shall die. And the Lord of hosts revealed Himself in mine ears, Surely this iniquity shall not be purged from you till ye die, saith the Lord, the Lord of hosts.

Here it is revealed to Isaiah that the iniquity of the inhabitants of Jerusalem shall not be purged until they die, and all the agonies of a protracted siege are represented as having been already endured. The rulers of the city have fled from the foe. its streets are full of the corpses of those who have died of famine, the hosts of Assyria occupy the valleys around it, and the people in their despair have drowned their fears in a last carousal, saying. 'Let us eat and drink, for to-morrow we die.' No part of this picture is applicable to the campaign of Sennacherib, when the Lord defended His city, so that the Assyrian shot not an arrow nor cast a bank against it. We can best explain the prophecy and the occasion that called it forth by combining the words of Isaiah with those of Sargon. and concluding that Sargon's conquest of Judah was not accomplished without the siege and capture of its capital. Ten years, therefore, before the campaign of Sennacherib, Jerusalem had felt the presence of an Assyrian army. a fact which serves to explain how it is that 'the 14th year' of Hezekiah has slipped into the text in Is. xxxvi. 1 (2 Kings xviii. 13) in place of 'the 24th.' It is remarkable, nevertheless, that so important an event should be unrecorded in the Book of Kings. Whatever the explanation of this may be, the incident is a curious and most interesting illustration of the way in which the recently discovered and translated Assyrian records tend to confirm and add to the Biblical historical records.

The fate of Merodach-baladan was now sealed. The year after the suppression of the revolt in the west (B.C. 710), Sargon hurled the whole power of the Assyrian empire against Babylonia. The Babylonian king made a vain effort to resist. His allies from Elam were driven back to their mountains, and Merodach-baladan himself was compelled to retreat to his ancestral marshes, leaving Babylon in the hands of the conqueror. Sargon now took the title of king of Babylonia; and though Merodach-baladan once more entered Babylon on the news of Sargon's death, his second reign was only of six months' duration, and Sennacherib eventually drove him out of the marshes where he had taken refuge, and forced him to find a new home on the shores of Elam. Even here, however, his followers were pursued by their merciless foe. In B.C. 697 Sennacherib manned a fleet with Phœnician sailors, and after pouring out libations to the gods of the Persian Gulf, sailed to the town the Chaldean prince had built, and utterly destroyed it. Babylonia might break from time to time into revolt, but after the fall of Merodach-baladan it ceased to be formidable.

Sargon was murdered in B.C. 705, and succeeded by his son Sennacherib. Brought up in the purple, Sennacherib soon showed that he was made of very different stuff from his father. Like the Persian Xerxes, he was weak and vainglorious, cowardly under reverse, cruel and boastful in success. Whether it was that his character was already known, or that the death of his father had inspired the vanquished enemies of Assyria with new hopes, we cannot say; certain it is that not only in Babylonia but also in the West the murder of Sargon was the signal for revolt against the Assyrian rule. Four years elapsed, however, before Sennacherib was ready to march against the rebels in Palestine. In B.C. 701 the campaign took place.

Hezekiah had placed himself at the head of a confederacy which included Phœnicia, Ammon, Moab, and Edom, and had the promised support of Tirhakah, the Ethiopian king of Egypt. His first act had been to secure the cities of the Philistines, always a thorn in the side of the Jewish kings. Padi, the king of Ekron, who led the Assyrian party, was carried to Jerusalem and there thrown into chains, while Ashkelon was placed under the government of a certain Zedekiah, whose name seems to imply his Jewish origin.

Sennacherib first fell upon the cities of the Phœnician coast. Sidon and other towns surrendered, and the Sidonian prince fled to the island of Cyprus. Pedael of Ammon, Chemosh-nadab of Moab, and Melech-ram of Edom came to offer homage and ask forgiveness from the Assyrian king, whose army now advanced to the south along the sea-shore. Leaving Jerusalem for the present, Sennacherib attacked Ashkelon, sent Zedekiah a prisoner to Nineveh, and placed the city under a vassal governor. The south of Judah was next ravaged, 200,150 of its inhabitants carried into captivity, and the important town of Lachish besieged and taken. The news of its capture reduced Hezekiah to despair. He sent ambassadors to the Assyrian camp, confessing that he had 'offended,' and offering to bear whatever burdens Sennacherib might impose upon him. Padi was sent back to Ekron, whose priests and nobles were put to death, and a gift of 30 talents of gold and 800 (or according to another standard of reckoning 300) talents of silver was offered by Hezekiah, along with the men of his body-guard, his eunuchs, his dancing-men and dancing-women, and the accumulated treasures of his palace. But Sennacherib was inexorable. He accepted the gifts indeed, but demanded besides that Hezekiah should surrender himself and his city. Nothing would suffice him save the possession of the strong fortress of Jerusalem and its conversion into the seat of an Assyrian satrap.

To this demand Hezekiah refused to accede. The advance of his ally Tirhakah from Egypt still held out a hope that the terrible invader might be compelled to return to his own land. That hope, however, was shattered at Eltekeh, where a battle took place which ended in the rout of the Egyptians, and nothing apparently intervened any longer between Hezekiah and his enemy except the walls of Jerusalem. Humanly speaking, the further resistance of the Jewish king was an act of folly and despair.

So at least thought Sennacherib and his officers, and a letter was despatched to Hezekiah requiring his submission, and declaring that the power of the Assyrian monarch was mightier than that of the God of Israel. But the letter brought with it the doom of its sender. Hezekiah entered the temple, and there on his knees, with the letter outspread before him, asked God to avenge the insult hurled at Him by the heathen, and to defend His city and people. The prayer was heard; and Isaiah was commissioned to declare that the Holy One of Israel would turn the Assyrian back by the way he had come, he should not enter Jerusalem 'nor shoot an arrow there, nor come before it with shields, nor cast a bank against it' (Is. xxxvii. 33).

The promise was not long in being fulfilled. 'The

angel of the Lord went forth, and smote in the camp of the Assyrians a hundred and fourscore and five thousand.' Sennacherib fled in haste from the scene of the disaster, carrying with him the prisoners and spoil he had swept from the south of Judah, along with the gifts with which Hezekiah had vainly essayed to buy off his threatened attack. 'The remnant' of Judah was saved, not by the help of the Egyptian king, not by alliances with the kingdoms of the West, not even by its own arm of flesh, but by the interposition of the Lord of Hosts.

Sennacherib never returned to Palestine. His rebellious vassal was allowed to conclude the five years that were left of his reign in peace. Jerusalem continued to be independent up to the time of Hezekiah's death. The year after his signal overthrow in Palestine the Assyrian monarch was occupied with affairs in Babylonia. The next year found him in Cilicia, and during the twenty years which elapsed between the Jewish campaign and his murder in B.C. 681 we never hear of his sending forth any more armies to the West. Indeed, the troubles and outbreaks that were constantly taking place in Babylonia kept him employed in the south, until he finally crushed all further opposition there by utterly destroying Babylon and choking the river Araxes with its ruins.

The murder of Sennacherib seems to have been occasioned by the favour he showed to his son Esar-haddon. Esar-haddon, however, justified this favour not only by defeating the parricides and their Armenian allies in a battle which decided the succession to the Assyrian throne, but also by the ability he displayed during the course of his reign. As a military commander he was in nowise inferior to his grandfather Sargon; as a civil administrator he proved himself the best of the Assyrian kings. His firm and conciliatory government effected what the wars of his predecessors had failed to achieve. He rebuilt Babylon, making it the second city of the empire, and induced the Babylonians to submit quietly to his rule. The princes of the West equally returned to their allegiance to Assyria; and although Manasseh of Judah was thrown into chains for disaffection he was subsequently released and restored to his kingdom [1]. From this time onwards there was no further attempt at revolt on the part of the Jewish kings; they acknowledged the supremacy of Assyria and paid their annual tribute, in return for which they were allowed to exercise undisputed sway over their Jewish subjects. But the Assyrian monarchs were secure against the hostility of the fortress of Jerusalem, and could use it as a base of operations in the event of a war with Egypt.

This war, in fact, was one of the leading features of Esar-haddon's reign, and ended in the Assyrian conquest of the country, which was partitioned into twenty satrapies. The war, as we have seen, seems to be foretold in outline in the 19th chapter of Isaiah. There God announces that He will set the Egyptians one against the other, 'city against city, kingdom against kingdom,' and will 'give them over into the hand of a cruel lord.' The prediction was literally fulfilled. The satrapies or kingdoms established by the Assyrians were constantly rising against their suzerain and warring against one another; Tirhakah from time to time emerged from his retreat in Ethiopia to lead the opposition against foreign rule, and the Assyrian king was obliged eventually to

[1] 2 Chron. xxxiii. 11–13.

E

take a terrible vengeance on Thebes or No-Amun. the ancient capital of Southern Egypt. Judah. from whence the invading armies poured. became a name of terror to the inhabitants of Egypt, and a day came when Judah and Egypt and Assyria alike formed parts of a single empire [1].

With the Assyrian conquest of Egypt Judah ceased to occupy the important position it had once held between the two rival powers of the ancient world. For awhile. therefore, its annals were uneventful. It was not until the decay of Assyria enabled the Egyptians to recover their independence and to revive the glories of their ancient dynasties, that the rulers of Jerusalem were once more called upon to play a part in the politics of Western Asia. When the final crash came, and the Babylonian empire of Nebuchadnezzar arose upon the ruins of Nineveh, Judah again found herself wedged in between two great hostile powers. But things had changed since the days of Hezekiah and Isaiah. Nebuchadnezzar was a more formidable foe than Sennacherib had been. and Jerusalem no longer had the choice of remaining neutral in the contest between Babylon and Egypt. It had to take its place on the one side or on the other, and that, too, not as a free state, but as a dependency which could call upon its suzerain to shield it from attack.

[1] Compare the prediction in Is. xix. 17.

CHAPTER IV.

THE kingdom of Syria, like the kingdom of Israel, had been carved out of the empire of David. Already in Solomon's lifetime the Syrian Rezon had established himself at Damascus, and there founded a monarchy which soon became formidable to its neighbours. It was more particularly with the adjoining kingdom of Israel that Damascus came into conflict. In the time of Baasha, Benhadad of Damascus made common cause with Asa against the northern kingdom, and the kings of Israel from Ahab onwards were constantly at war with the Syrian princes. It was only when a common danger threatened Damascus and Israel alike that we find Ahab sending 2000 chariots and 10,000 men to Hadadezer of Damascus, to assist him against Assyrian attack; and, though the Israelites had by treaty a bazaar in the Syrian capital [1], it required a renewal of the Assyrian invasions to unite Israel and Syria again. Indeed, the capture and plunder of Damascus by the Assyrians in B.C. 804 was taken advantage of by Jeroboam II to 'restore the coast of Israel from the entering of Hamath unto the sea of the plain.'

But the revival of Assyrian power under Tiglath-pileser brought with it an important change in the political

---

[1] 1 Kings xx. 34. See also Amos iii. 12.

E 2

relations of the West.   The league between Syria and
Israel, brought about by the invasion of Shalmaneser II
in the time of Ahab, was renewed by Rezon [1], the last
king of Damascus, and Pekah, the Israelitish usurper.   It
was again the pressure of an Assyrian invasion which
created the alliance.   The tribute Tiglath-pileser had
forced upon Menahem proved that a power more
dangerous even than that of Shalmaneser had arisen in
the East, and that it was time for the princes of the
West to save themselves from the threatening attack by
common action.

The kingdom of Israel had been founded by usurpation,
and its history is that of a line of usurpers.   The dynasty
of its founder lasted but a short while.   His son was
murdered during the siege of a Philistine fortress by one
of his own generals, who thereupon seized the crown.
The precedent thus set was followed time after time.
Murder and usurpation led the way to the throne.
Omri and Jehu alone contrived to hand down their
power for more than one generation, and with the
murder of Zechariah, the last descendant of Jehu, all
semblance of any other title to the crown than that of
successful revolt came to an end.   The government of
Samaria became the prey of the strongest or most
popular commander.

Like the second Assyrian empire, therefore, the
Israelitish kingdom was founded on military violence,
but, unlike the second Assyrian empire, it produced no

---

[1] The Assyrian inscriptions show that we must read Rezon instead of
Rezin in those passages of the Old Testament in which the Syrian king
is named.   Rezon had been the name of the founder of the kingdom of
Damascus (1 Kings xi. 23), and we find the same interchange of *u* or *o* and *i*
in the names of Tou (1 Chron. xviii. 9) by the side of Toi, and of Huram
2 Chron. ii. 11, by the side of Hiram.

Sargon to establish a permanent dynasty. It was the creation of the army rather than of the people; its rulers could claim none of the *prestige* and respect that comes from ancient descent, or show any better title for their power than that of successful rebellion. It is little wonder, therefore, that they found themselves at the mercy of every revolution in the army, and that an ambitious or discontented general considered he had as good a right to the crown as its actual possessor. The result was constant change and civil war, a development of the military spirit which absorbed all else, and the exaltation of the military commander above his king. The bond which bound the tribes together ceased to be either national or religious, and became purely military. It was to the general of the army, rather than to the representative of the nation and its faith, that obedience was paid. When the military organisation was broken up which had connected them together, the Israelitish tribes at once fell apart; they had no national life, no traditions of glorious deeds achieved under an ancient line of kings, no religious worship associated with the name of a royal house and a central shrine. The overthrow of Samaria by the Assyrians meant the complete obliteration of the Israelitish tribes as a nation. Those who were carried into exile were lost among the peoples in the midst of whom they were settled; those who remained at home were absorbed into the older Canaanite population or else united themselves with the Jews[1].

[1] Thus in St. Luke ii. 36, it is stated that Anna was 'of the tribe of Aser,' and we learn from 2 Chron. xxx., xxxi., that after the overthrow of the kingdom of Samaria 'all Israel' was united with Judah in a common government and faith. As we have seen above, the number of captives carried away from Samaria by Sargon was but small.

To all this the history of the monarchy of Judah offers
a complete contrast. Here we find a stable government,
an unbroken line of princes who traced their descent
from the time-honoured names of David and Solomon,
and a religious worship that had its seat in a central
sanctuary. While in Israel all was division. in Judah all
was unity. In place of ten different tribes. some of
whom were separated from the others by the valley of
the Jordan. Judah formed a homogeneous whole. The
tribe of Simeon had been absorbed. the Levites were
a religious order. and the differences that once existed
between Judah and Benjamin had been healed by the
position of the capital. which stood partly in the territory
of the one. and partly in the territory of the other.
Instead of the military revolutions which were incessantly
giving new dynasties to the northern kingdom. the sceptre
of Judah was quietly handed down from father to son. In
Judah there was one capital. one temple. one recognised
form of faith : in Israel. on the contrary. the capital was
shifted from Shechem to Tirzah. and from Tirzah to
Samaria : there were at least two rival sanctuaries at
Dan and Beth-el. and the worship of the Baalim of
Canaan struggled for the mastery against a corrupt
worship of the God of Israel.

In Judah. moreover, revolt was not consecrated by
success and custom. Around the royal house gathered
all the memories of the past, and each generation saw
the house of David knit by closer bonds of habit and
tradition to the people over whom it ruled. Nor did it
stand in the same antagonism to the prophets and the
prophetical schools as the usurpers of the Samaritan
crown. Ahab. it is true, had his prophets who prophesied
to him smooth things, but the true prophets of God were

at bitter enmity with his house, and an Amos, or a Hosea, though they might be born in the kingdom of Israel, turned their eyes not to their own land, but to that of Judah. Ephraim, says Hosea, compasseth the Lord ' about with lies, and the house of Israel with deceit ; but Judah yet ruleth with God, and is faithful with the saints[1].' They looked forward to the day when the children of Israel should ' return, and seek the Lord their God, and David their king[2].' Even Judah, however, was not wholly free from the disaffected and factious : no kingdom has ever been, more especially a kingdom of the ancient world. From time to time the weakness or worthlessness of the ruler favoured an outbreak of discontent, which ended, as in the case of Amon, with the murder of the reigning prince. But even in such a case the majority of the nation clung loyally to their royal house. Amon might be conspired against and slain by his servants, but ' the people of the land' at once punished the conspirators and set the son of the murdered king upon his father's throne. The people of Judah had not learnt, like the people of Israel, that might is right ; the successful usurpers of Samaria would never have caused their title to be acknowledged in the southern kingdom.

The house of David was perhaps never so weak, had never so far lost its hold upon the affections of the people, as at the time when Pekah and Rezon formed their league against the encroachments of Assyria. The leprosy of Uzziah, which cut him off from intercourse with his kind, and the long regency of Jotham, had sapped that feeling of personal loyalty towards the reigning sovereign which is so necessary to an Oriental

[1] Hosea xi. 12.　　　　[2] Hosea iii. 5.

government. There was no visible king ruling over the
nation ; the real king was invisible to his subjects, and
though his representative might be the heir-apparent he
was not yet invested with the mysterious power and
dignity that accompanied the name of king.

Uzziah must have died but a very short while before
his son Jotham. In B. C. 742 he had been compelled to
purchase peace from Tiglath-pileser by the offer of submission and the payment of tribute, and it was only
eight years later, in B. C. 734, that his grandson Ahaz
was imploring the Assyrian monarch to protect him
against his Syrian and Israelitish foes. Ahaz was but
twenty years old when he succeeded his father, and the
respect for the throne which had been weakened by the
long regency of Jotham was further impaired by the
youthful age of his son. ' As for my people,' says Isaiah[1],
' children are their oppressors, and women rule over
them.' The rule of the harem was characteristic of the
reign of a young prince.

The last days of Jotham, moreover. had been disturbed
by the approach of an aggressive war. He seems to
have adhered faithfully to his father's pact with Tiglath-
pileser ; at all events, the kingdom of Judah, alone
among the populations of Palestine, refused to take part
in the defensive league against the Assyrians. Ammon
and Moab, Edom and the Philistines—who were ever on
the watch for an opportunity of shaking off the government of their suzerain the Jewish king—all joined the
Syro-Israelitish confederacy ; Judah alone stood aloof.
The confederates, accordingly, determined to displace
the reigning dynasty and to substitute for it a creature
of their own. For the first time the attack made upon

[1] Is. iii. 12.

Judah by its northern neighbours was made not against
the country itself, but against its rulers ; it was the overthrow of the house of David, not the conquest of Judah,
which was the object they had in view. It is probable
that the new king who was destined for the Jewish throne
was not of Jewish extraction ; he is called the son of
Tabeel, or more correctly Tabel (Isaiah vii. 6), and the
resemblance of this name to that of the Syrian Tab-
Rimmon gives colour to the belief that he was one of the
subjects of Rezon. In any case, if once he could have
been introduced within Jerusalem, the allies would have
been able to control and direct the policy of Judah.

The assailants could count upon the support of a party
in the midst of Judah itself. Isaiah (viii. 6) denounces
the people who ' refuseth the waters of Shiloah that go
softly, and rejoice in Rezin and Remaliah's son,' and
declares that they shall be punished hereafter by the
flood of the Assyrian invasion. Those who had been
alienated by the worthlessness of Ahaz and his favourites,
and those who belonged to the Egyptian or anti-Assyrian
party, all favoured the designs of the enemies of Ahaz.
He stood in the way of their joining the common alliance
with Egypt and the surrounding nations against Assyria ;
his rule and character were alike contemptible, and
therefore they would have him away. But the mass of
the people stood firm ; like the priests and prophets, they
tolerated the sins and follies of Ahaz for the sake of
' David his father,' and the royal house of which he was
the representative ; and they refused to merge their
kingdom and nationality in the heathen populations which
dwelt around them. Though defeated in the field, the
subjects of Ahaz still held out behind the strong walls
of Jerusalem, and in the moment of extremest danger

Isaiah went forth to encourage him with a message from the Lord.

The position of Ahaz was indeed a perilous one. His forces were broken; his capital was threatened with siege, he was surrounded on all sides by formidable enemies, while there were traitors within his own camp. We need not wonder if, under these circumstances, he and his councillors hurried to Assyria for help. It was on account of their faithfulness to Tiglath-pileser that the troubles they were encountering had come upon them, and there was no other powerful ally to whom they could turn. Egypt was on the side of their enemies; in Palestine itself all was hostile.

It was now when Ahaz had gone forth to examine the defences of Jerusalem that Isaiah met him with a message from the God of Israel. The prophet enjoined him not to fear nor to be 'faint-hearted for the two tails of the smoking firebrands' of Samaria and Syria: the Syro-Israelitish alliance should be broken up, and Damascus and Ephraim should alike be destroyed. All the Jewish king was required to do was to remain 'quiet': God would see that the confederacy against him should not succeed [1].

Ahaz, however, had already determined upon his policy. He had too little faith in the prophet's message to await the issue in trustful confidence, and ambassadors had already been despatched to the Assyrian monarch, calling upon him to succour his faithful vassal. Ahaz refused, accordingly, to test whether or not the words and advice of Isaiah were from the Lord, and brought down upon himself the denunciation of the doom that his faithlessness had merited. Upon him and his house

---

[1] Is. vii. 9.

and his people it was declared the Assyrian should indeed come, not as a deliverer, but as an oppressor, wasting and destroying the land until it became desolate of inhabitants and devoid of cultivation.

Advice and denunciation were equally lost upon the king. Ahaz followed his own policy, and acknowledged himself the vassal of Assyria. 'I am thy servant and thy son,' were the words his ambassadors were instructed to repeat to Tiglath-pileser, and the act of homage was sealed by the heavy tribute they carried with them. The policy at first seemed successful. The enemies of Ahaz had themselves to struggle for their lives. Damascus and Samaria were besieged and taken, and both Rezon and Pekah were put to death. The Syro-Israelitish league was at an end; its authors had perished, and Judah had never again any reason to fear either Damascus or Israel.

But in bringing the Assyrian upon Palestine, Ahaz had not only placed himself and his successors at the feet of a foreign monarch; he had opened the way for Assyria into the West, and had caused the natural barriers between his kingdom and the Assyrian power to be swept away. Henceforward Judah and Assyria stood face to face; there was no longer a Damascus or a Samaria to bear the brunt of a first attack. The consequences of the policy of Ahaz soon made themselves felt in the reign of his son, and brought upon Judah the invasions first of Sargon and then of Sennacherib. His subjects had good reason to regret that Ahaz had not listened to Isaiah. and awaited in quietude and faith the issue of events.

The Syrian kingdom ceased to exist. Its population was transported to Kir, and Damascus became the seat of an Assyrian satrap. As a political factor Syria was wiped out of the history of the West.

Samaria was of less importance than Damascus in the eyes of Tiglath-pileser. Whereas Damascus stood a two years' siege, Samaria fell at once into his hands. It is therefore probable that there was in Israel an Assyrian party, or at all events a party opposed to Pekah, the leader of which was Hoshea. While, therefore, Pekah was executed, and the trans-Jordanic tribes, as being nearest to Damascus, were carried into captivity, the kingdom of Samaria was allowed to continue under the government of Hoshea. But Hoshea soon found his position as a tributary vassal of Assyria too irksome to be endured. The death of Tiglath-pileser seemed a favourable opportunity for throwing off the yoke and for turning to Egypt for support. The Phœnician cities asserted their independence at the same time, and Shalmaneser the Assyrian king besieged Tyre during all the five years of his reign without success. He was, however, more successful in Israel. Hoshea was deposed and thrown into chains, and the Israelitish throne remained vacant for ever. For three years longer the governing classes of Samaria held out, in the vain hope of Egyptian succour; Samaria fell, as Damascus had fallen before, and the kingdom of Jeroboam, like the kingdom of Syria, passed away. It would appear that more than once subsequently its inhabitants attempted to free themselves from Assyrian authority. The colonists from Hamath and Babylonia could not have settled in the country until after Sargon's conquest of Hamath in B.C. 720, and of Babylonia in B.C. 710; and we gather from Ezra iv. 2, 10, that Asnapper or Assur-bani-pal, the son of Esar-haddon, planted other colonists

from Elam there at a still later date. It was then that
the prediction in Isaiah vii. 8 found its final accomplishment; 'within threescore and five years' after the assault
upon Judah, Ephraim was broken and ceased to be a
people. In the closing days of the Assyrian empire,
when the central authority had grown feeble, and could
no longer assert its power in the distant dependencies,
we find Josiah exercising his sway over what had once
been the territory of the revolted tribes. In the evening
of the house of David the kingdom of David and Solomon
was again restored to their descendants; the schism
made by Jeroboam was healed, and the remnant of
Israel once more acknowledged the same head as Judah.
But it was a remnant only; the policy of Pekah had
resulted in the destruction not only of himself. but also
of his city and his people.

CHAPTER V.

WE have now finished our survey of the states and powers by which Judah was surrounded in the days of Isaiah, and of the events which were influencing for good or for ill the political fortunes of God's people. It is time to turn to Judah itself, to trace the effects of these events upon the prophet's countrymen, and to see how, under divine guidance, they were working towards the training and purification of the Jewish race.

The lifetime of Isaiah witnessed a complete revolution in the politics of Western Asia, a revolution which ushered in a new world and closed for ever the book of the past. During his early years Western Asia was still what it had been for unnumbered centuries—a collection of small states, some of them indeed at times sufficiently formidable to their neighbours, but none of them powerful or ambitious enough to swallow up the rest. Then came the rise of the second Assyrian empire, and the new conception on the part of its founders of a centralised power which should rule supreme in the civilised East. The greater part of Isaiah's life was spent in watching the sure though gradual realisation of this new idea. But before his death the check received in Palestine by Sennacherib introduced a change into the mode and method of realising it, and obliged the Assyrian government to pause in its career of conquest. It became obvious that the conquered populations could not be forced into unity; the Assyrian kings might transplant them to other regions of the empire, and fill the thrones of their princes with tributary satraps; but the spirit of rebellion and discontent still survived, and the unity of the empire was only apparent, not real. Mere force could not effect that imperial organisation which the rulers of Nineveh aimed at, or fuse the dis-united units into a single whole. Conquest must be followed by a policy of conciliation, the feelings of the vanquished must be respected, and not trampled on.

While, therefore, Sargon and Sennacherib were em-ployed in extending the empire and carrying out the dreams of Tiglath-pileser by brute force, it was reserved for Esar-haddon to consolidate their conquests by a milder administration and fuller permission for the development of the national life. The vanquished nations were no longer compelled to become Assyrians and to acknowledge Assur as their god; they were allowed to retain their old habits and customs, their old religion, even their old form of government. In place of the satraps the native kings were allowed to preserve their sway over the subject populations; Manasseh of Judah was as much a servant of 'the great king' as the Assyrian governor of Samaria, but so long as he acknowledged the supremacy of Nineveh and paid the annual tribute he was allowed to govern his people after the fashion of his fathers. It was only where the older lines of rulers had been replaced by satraps before the change took place in the imperial policy that the order of things established by Sennacherib and his predecessors con-tinued to prevail; elsewhere, in Judah, in Edom, in the petty principalities of Egypt, the government was left in the hands of the native princes.

Isaiah, it is true, did not live to see this change of policy fully carried out. He died during the short breathing-space that followed the overthrow of Sennacherib's army, while Judah again enjoyed a brief season of independence; but he must have foreseen the approaching change, and have recognised that here too the safety of Judah lay, not in revolt and foreign intrigue, but in quietude and submission.

It was natural that the Jewish statesmen should be slow in understanding the profound change which Tiglath-pileser and his successors were effecting in the condition and politics of the Oriental world. Assyria was a country of which they had hitherto heard little or nothing; their statecraft had hitherto been exercised in petty wars against the Philistines or the Edomites, or in warding off an attack of some Israelitish king. However much misery might be inflicted for the moment by the invasions of their neighbours, it soon passed away; no attempt was made to destroy their national existence, and even the capture of Jerusalem by Jehoash [1] brought with it nothing worse than the plunder of the palace and temple and the destruction of a part of the city wall. Their own arms were matched against those of populations hardly more numerous or more powerful than themselves, and the vicissitudes of war as often brought them victory as defeat. The politics of Palestine were necessarily on a small scale; its wars were petty and of little lasting effect; and the relations of the several states one to another were like those of the Heptarchy in the earlier history of our own country. The only power of magnitude and wealth which came within their horizon was Egypt; and the glories and might of Egypt

[1] Kings xiv. 13, 14.

had long become a matter of tradition only. Egypt was an excellent neighbour for the purposes of trade ; its unwarlike population excited no feeling of insecurity in the minds of the inhabitants of Palestine.

The sudden rise and onward march of Assyria, accordingly, came upon its politicians like a thunder-clap. Ahaz and his councillors realised but little what this new portent in Oriental history signified. Had they done so, they would never have rushed, as they did, into the destroyer's arms ; Syria and Ephraim might seem formidable for the moment, but Assyria was formidable in the future. Isaiah vainly endeavoured to warn them of the perils they were bringing on their country, but they would not listen. As yet the power of Assyria was like a cloud no bigger than a man's hand.

Hezekiah inherited the results of his father's policy. By this time the statesmen of Palestine were fully awake to the dangers by which they were menaced. The lesson taught by the overthrow of Damascus and Samaria, of Arpad and Hamath, was not soon to be forgotten. But they could not shake off the influence of old habits and traditions. In their hour of need they turned to Egypt for help. Like Assyria, Egypt had revived under an Ethiopian king ; it was once more a united and prosperous power, and the memory of a past age, when Egypt was the one great power known to the nations of the East, produced an exaggerated idea of its strength and importance. Assyria might be powerful, but Egypt, it was believed, was equally powerful, and, if it chose to move, could drive the Assyrian hordes back to their home beyond the Euphrates.

The Egyptian party was consequently numerous in Jerusalem. They urged the necessity of looking to

F

Egypt for support, and of resisting the attack of the Assyrians with Egyptian help. Their policy, indeed, seemed at once natural and patriotic. Submission to Assyria meant not only national degradation, but national annihilation as well; all that the Rab-shakeh of Sennacherib could promise the people of Jerusalem if they surrendered to him was transportation to another clime. On the other hand, alliance with Egypt would leave the Jewish king on a footing of equality with the Egyptian monarch; the gifts carried by the ambassadors of Judah were merely the customary offerings of one potentate to another, and implied no act of homage, no acknowledgment of inferiority. Moreover, an Egyptian invasion was not to be thought of; the Egyptians had no desire to absorb the territories of others, and the Ethiopian king was fully occupied in maintaining his own authority. Without help, the hundreds of Judah must succumb to the thousands of Assyria; the power which had swept away the mighty kingdom of Damascus would not be turned back by 'the remnant of Zion.'

The leader of the Egyptian party seems to have been Shebna. From the termination of his name, we may infer that he was of Syrian descent, a fact which gives point to Isaiah's denunciation of the arrogant stranger who had dared to hew his sepulchre out of the cliffs reserved for the royal lineage of David[1] :—

Thus saith the Lord, the Lord of hosts, Go, get thee unto this treasurer, even unto Shebna, which is over the house, and say, What doest thou here? and whom hast thou here, that thou hast hewed thee out here a sepulchre? hewing him out a sepulchre on high, graving an habitation for himself in the rock! Behold, the Lord will hurl thee away violently as a strong man; yea, He will wrap

[1] Isa. xxii. 15-25.

thee up closely. He will surely turn and toss thee like a ball into a large country ; there shalt thou die, and there shall be the chariots of thy glory, thou shame of thy lord's house. And I will thrust thee from thine office, and from thy station shall He pull thee down. And it shall come to pass in that day, that I will call My servant Eliakim the son of Hilkiah : and I will clothe him with thy robe, and strengthen him with thy girdle, and I will commit thy government into his hand : and he shall be a father to the inhabitants of Jerusalem, and to the house of Judah. And the key of the house of David will I lay upon his shoulder ; and he shall open, and none shall shut ; and he shall shut, and none shall open. And I will fasten him as a nail in a sure place ; and he shall be for a throne of glory to his father's house. And they shall hang upon him all the glory of his father's house, the offspring and the issue, every small vessel, from the vessels of cups even to all the vessels of flagons In that day, saith the Lord of hosts, shall the nail that was fastened in a sure place give way ; and it shall be hewn down, and fall, and the burden that was upon it shall be cut off ; for the Lord hath spoken it.

This is the only case in which the prophet utters a prophecy against an individual ; but Shebna represented a party and a policy, and in predicting the fate of the leader, Isaiah predicted also the fate of the policy. During a considerable part of Hezekiah's reign the king shared the views of Shebna, who accordingly governed in his name. As in modern Turkey, the removal of the vizier indicated a change in the policy of the king ; when Shebna was replaced by Eliakim, it meant that the policy identified with the name of Shebna had been forsaken by Hezekiah. Eliakim, we may gather from the words of Isaiah, was a God-fearing man, willing to hearken to the prophet's advice and warning. Already, when the Rab-shakeh appeared before Jerusalem, we find that Shebna had been overthrown ; Eliakim had been raised to the viziership, and Shebna degraded to the

position of scribe. It may be that the approach of
Sennacherib, unimpeded by the armies of Egypt, had
opened the eyes of Hezekiah; at all events, from hence-
forth the policy of those who urged alliance and union
with the bruised reed of Egypt received no more
countenance from the Jewish king.

Opposed to the Egyptian was the Assyrian party,
which advocated submission to the all-powerful empire
of Assyria. It may be questioned whether the party
was ever a very large one: certainly it never appears to
have influenced the policy of the government after
the death of Ahaz. Doubtless its partisans had been
active and sufficiently numerous during the reign of
a king whose policy had been shaped by their coun-
sels; but events had shaken its influence, and it is
probable that it numbered but few adherents after
the fall of Samaria. A patriotic Jew, in fact, could
hardly advise his countrymen to take upon their necks
the yoke of Assyria without, at least, making some
struggle for independence. The empire of Assyria
was not yet sufficiently consolidated in the West for
such a struggle to seem altogether hopeless. As soon
as it was discovered that submission to Assyria meant
the loss of national freedom, its advocates must have
become fewer and fewer, until at last they all dwindled
away. Though the Rab-shakeh of Sennacherib addressed
the people of Jerusalem in their own language, at a time
when the condition of the kingdom appeared wellnigh
desperate, there was none found among them to answer
him a word. There was none who proposed surrender:
all were willing to resist the invader up to the last.

A third party, which we may call national, was headed
by Isaiah. It drew its policy and its existence from the

words of Divine counsel which the prophet uttered, and the message he was commissioned to deliver. Its watchword was 'quietness and rest'; 'in returning and rest shall ye be saved, in quietness and confidence shall be your strength [1].' It was a policy of non-intervention, that was opposed to an alliance with Assyria or Egypt; Judah had gained nothing but evil from intermeddling with the politics of its heathen neighbours, its religion and morality had been corrupted, and calamity after calamity had fallen on the nation. God had marked it out as 'a peculiar people,' and its safety lay in the national recognition of the fact. It was He who had permitted the Assyrian to be the rod of His anger, and had allowed him to chastise and chasten the sins of His people; but the chastisement was not to be utter destruction, and a bound had been set beyond which the violence of the invader was not to go. A remnant was yet to escape from Zion. and the Assyrian should be beaten down 'which smote with a rod [2].'

Isaiah preached for long to deaf ears. Ahaz turned for help to the Assyrian, Hezekiah to the Egyptian. King and people alike could not believe that the Lord would interfere on behalf of His city, and overthrow the foe in the very moment of his success. Hezekiah might accept the rebuke of the prophet for his pride of heart in showing the ambassadors of Babylon the treasures of his house. but he did not forsake the policy he was following, and cease to plot with Egypt and Babylonia against the Assyrian king. Even the conquest of Judah by Sargon did not open the eyes of the king and his councillors. Their envoys made their way up the Nile to arrange fresh alliances with the Ethiopian ruler

---

[1] Isa. xxx. 15. [2] Isa. x. 21, 24, 27.

of Egypt. and Judah placed herself at the head of a league which comprised all the states of the West. It needed the campaign of Sennacherib and the signal deliverance of Jerusalem from the victorious enemy to convince Hezekiah that Egypt should indeed 'help in vain,' and that the true policy of himself and his country was that which had so long been pressed upon them by Isaiah. If he and his people would trust in the Lord, and abstain from all intrigues with foreign powers, they might rest in peace and safety, for the Lord Himself would defend them in the hour of need.

After the rise of the second Assyrian empire. therefore, and the changed conditions it introduced into the politics of Western Asia, three parties formed themselves in Judah, each of which directed in succession the affairs of the kingdom. The pressure of the Syro-Ephraimitic war created the Assyrian party, and led to its predominance throughout the reign of Ahaz. The overthrow of Samaria. which brought Judah and Assyria into immediate contact. as well as the growing fear of the power of Nineveh. caused this party to fall with the death of the king. Hezekiah and his advisers now threw themselves into the hands of the Egyptian party, whose leader we may see in Shebna. Its influence was marked by revolt from Assyria, by alliance with Egypt. and by attempts to create a league against the Assyrians among the neighbouring states. The cities of the Philistines, forming as they did a link between Egypt and Judah, assumed increased importance; the old suzerainty which the Jewish kings claimed over them was asserted more forcibly than before, and their princes were made and unmade in accordance with the dictates of Jewish policy. The defeat of Tirhakah at Eltekeh shattered the power of the Egyptian party; Shebna was succeeded as vizier by Eliakim, and the views and teachings of Isaiah were at last allowed to prevail. For the rest of Hezekiah's life Isaiah was his political as well as his religious counsellor; the lesson taught by the terrible invasion of Sennacherib was never forgotten. And though with the death of Hezekiah evil days came again upon Judah—days which, we may gather, Isaiah was privileged never to see—the effect of the prophet's policy continued to be felt. The house of David and the national existence of the people over whom it ruled were preserved until a new king arose in Assyria and inaugurated new principles of government. The temple and kingdom of Jerusalem were saved till the time was ripe for the chosen people to pass through the fiery ordeal of the Babylonish exile.

The political revolution of which the Oriental world was the scene during the lifetime of Isaiah could not be without its influence on the life and thoughts of the Jewish people. To the intercourse of Ahaz with Tiglath-pileser we must trace the introduction of Babylonian science into Jerusalem and the literary revival that distinguished his son's reign. As we have seen, the sun-dial of Ahaz is an unmistakable illustration of Babylonian influence, like the library which we find existing in the days of Hezekiah in imitation of the libraries of Babylonia and Nineveh. The enlarged political horizon, moreover, brought with it new knowledge and new interests. Judah ceased to be one out of many small and unimportant states; it became the centre around which for several years the fate of Western Asia seemed to turn, the battle-ground between the two great powers which represented the present and the past. Perforce, therefore, its inhabitants were compelled to understand

and follow the fortunes of their neighbours from the
Tigris to the Nile, and to know as much about Babylon
or Ethiopia as they had once known about Edom and
Damascus. The results of this enlargement of the
political sphere showed itself in many ways. Jerusalem
became a fortress the walls of which needed to be
strengthened with all the engineering skill of the day.
The Assyrian enemy it was called upon to resist was a
very different one from the Samaritan king who had
once penetrated within it [1]. But it is more particularly
in the domain of prophecy that we see the influence of
the new order of things. In the hands of Isaiah and his
contemporaries prophecy becomes universal, extending
its range of vision far beyond the narrow boundaries of
the Israelitish tribes. It is not only Jerusalem or
Samaria upon which 'the burden' of the prophetic vision
falls; Egypt, Assyria, Ethiopia, even Babylon and the
distant Elam come within its scope. Their fortunes are
now intimately bound up with those of God's people; if
Israel is God's inheritance, Egypt is His people, and
Assyria the work of His hands [2].

The position occupied by Isaiah was necessitated by
the age to which he belonged. The message he com-
municated was in accordance with the conditions of his
time. Hence arises the striking contrast between the
policy of which he was the mouthpiece, and that which
Jeremiah was called upon to urge. While Isaiah advocated resistance to the invader, in confident security that
God would defend His temple and city, Jeremiah
declared that no buildings made with hands could save
the people, and that submission to the Chaldean was
their only hope of safety. Isaiah, in other words, was the

---

[1] 2 Kings xiv. 13.   [2] Is. xix. 25.

prophet of national independence, Jeremiah of national subjection. But between the time of Isaiah and that of Jeremiah a total change had come over the face of the Eastern world. Nebuchadnezzar was a more dangerous enemy than Sennacherib; Egypt had risen afresh from its ashes, and was prepared to reassert its ancient rule over Palestine, and Judah itself had sunk into the deepest degradation and decay. Its princes were idolatrous and corrupt, and Nebuchadnezzar himself was a more reverent observer of the moral law than they. The measure of Judah's iniquities was full: the period of God's longsuffering had drawn to a close, and there was no king on the throne like Hezekiah to follow loyally the teachings of the prophet, no minister like Eliakim to carry them out. The Lord would fight no longer for His city and the earthly throne of David : His people were to be disciplined by suffering, and to be taught that the Most High dwelleth not in temples made with hands, but requires truth and uprightness, not correctness of ritual or stately shrines.

Had the kingdom of Judah been swept away by the Assyrian kings, like the kingdom of Samaria, it is doubtful whether there would have been any 'remnant' to return to it again. It needed another century to produce in Judah a body of men sufficiently numerous and faithful to the God of their fathers to withstand the allurements of the idolatry around them. When Sennacherib threatened Jerusalem, the reforms of Hezekiah were but just accomplished, the more far-reaching reformation of Josiah had not taken place. The Jewish people had but just ceased to burn incense in the temple itself to the brazen serpent of Moses [1], the

---

[1] 2 Kings xviii. 4.

high-places were still frequented by those who believed
themselves the true worshippers of the Lord, and the
Assyrian envoy could appeal to the indignation and
resentment which the destruction of these ancient sanctuaries by Hezekiah had aroused in the hearts of his
subjects [1]. Literature and education were taking a new
start, the utterances of the prophets were but just beginning to be written down, and so preserved as a testimony
for ever, and the religious ignorance even of the priests
may be judged of by the fact that the book of the Law
was not found in the temple until the reign of Josiah.
The religious training of the chosen people was still in-
complete : a few good men might have kept the light of
truth burning in the land of their captivity for a time,
but as they passed away the whole body of the exiles
would have been merged as completely in the nations
among whom they lived as were the captive Israelites.
Nor would the Assyrian Exile have had a speedy ending,
like the Babylonian Exile. Instead of seventy years, it
would have been nearly two centuries before the captives
would have been released from their house of bondage ;
when Nineveh fell, there was no Cyrus to restore its
prisoners to their old homes.

The policy, then, which Isaiah was empowered to
press upon his countrymen, the promises he was commissioned to hold out, were adapted to other circumstances and other needs than those which confronted
Jeremiah. The object and end of both prophets was the
same, but the means for effecting the end were necessarily
different. Jeremiah lived when the old national independence with its Oriental court and foreign alliances
had ceased to be possible or desirable ; Isaiah's lot was

---

[1] 2 Kings xviii. 22.

cast in a happier age, when the safe-keeping of Jerusalem
was needful to the divine education of the people of the
Lord.   He had the privilege of leading the national
struggle against foreign oppression and heathen arro-
gance, of promising success to his countrymen in their
supreme hour of peril, and of seeing that promise fulfilled.   The hosts of the Assyrian, which none had yet
been able to resist, were shattered against the walls of
Jerusalem, and Isaiah's had been the voice of the herald
which announced the doom of the enemies of Israel.

APPENDIX.

—••—

I.

'The towns of Gil(ead) and Abel-(beth-Maachah) in the provinces of Beth-Omri [Samaria], the widespread (district of Naph-
ta)li to its whole extent I turned into the territory of Assyria. My
(governors) and officers I appointed (over them). Khanun of
Gaza, who had fled before my weapons, escaped (to the land) of
Egypt. The city of Gaza (his royal city I captured. Its spoils
and) its gods (I carried away. My name) and the image of my
majesty (I set up) in the midst of the temple of . . . The gods
of their land I counted (as a spoil). . . To his land I restored him
and (imposed tribute upon him. Gold), silver, garments of damask
and linen (along with other objects) I received. The land of Beth-
Omri (I overran). A selection of its inhabitants (with their goods)
I transported to Assyria. Pekah their king I put to death, and
I appointed Hoshea to the sovereignty over them. Ten (talents of
gold, . . . talents of silver as) their tribute I received, and I transported them to Assyria.'

II.

I. '(In the beginning of my reign) the city of Samaria I besieged,
I captured ; 27,280 of its inhabitants I carried away: fifty chariots
in the midst of them I collected, and the rest of their goods I
seized ; I set my governor over them and laid upon them the
tribute of the former king (Hoshea).'

II. '(In my ninth expedition and eleventh year) the people of
the Philistines, Judah, Edom, and Moab, who dwell by the sea,
who owed tribute and presents to Assur my lord, plotted rebellion,
men of insolence, who in order to revolt against me carried their

bribes for alliance to Pharaoh king of Egypt, a prince who could not save them, and sent him homage. I, Sargon, the established prince, the reverer of the worship of Assur and Merodach, the protector of the renown of Assur, caused the warriors who belonged to me entirely to pass the rivers Tigris and Euphrates during full flood, and that same Yavan (of Ashdod) their king, who trusted in his (forces) and did not (reverence) my sovereignty, heard of the progress of my expedition to the land of the Hittites (Syria), and the fear of (Assur) my (lord) overwhelmed him, and to the borders of Egypt . . . he fled away.'

III.

SENNACHERIB'S ACCOUNT OF HIS CAMPAIGN AGAINST JUDAH.

'ZEDEKIAH, king of Ashkelon, who had not submitted to my yoke, himself, the gods of the house of his fathers, his wife, his sons, his daughters and his brothers, the seed of the house of his fathers, I removed, and I sent him to Assyria. I set over the men of Ashkelon Sarludari, the son of Rukipti, their former king, and I imposed upon him the payment of tribute, and the homage due to my majesty, and he became a vassal. In the course of my campaign I approached and captured Beth-Dagon, Joppa, Bene-berak and Azur, the cities of Zedekiah, which did not submit at once to my yoke, and I carried away their spoil. The priests, the chief men and the common people of Ekron, who had thrown into chains their king, Padi, because he was faithful to his oaths to Assyria, and had given him up to Hezekiah, the Jew, who imprisoned him in hostile fashion in a dark dungeon, feared in their hearts. The king of Egypt, the bowmen, the chariots and the horses of the king of Ethiopia, had gathered together innumerable forces and gone to their assistance. In sight of the town of Eltekeh was their order of battle drawn up; they summoned their troops (to the battle). Trusting in Assur, my lord, I fought with them and overthrew them. My hands took the captains of the chariots and the sons of the king of Egypt, as well as the captains of the chariots of the king of Ethiopia, alive in the midst of the battle. I approached and captured the towns of Eltekeh and Timnath, and I carried away their spoil. I marched against the city of Ekron, and put to death the priests and the chief men who had committed the sin (of rebellion), and I hung up their bodies on stakes all round the city. The citizens who had done wrong and wickedness I counted as spoil; as for the rest of them who had committed no sin or crime, in whom no fault was found, I proclaimed their freedom (from punishment). I had Padi, their king, brought out from the midst of Jerusalem, and I seated him on the throne of royalty over them, and I laid upon him the tribute due to my majesty. But as for Hezekiah of Judah, who had not submitted to my yoke, forty-six of his strong cities, together with innumerable fortresses and small towns which depended on them, by overthrowing the walls and open attack, by battle, engines and battering-rams I besieged, I captured. I brought out from the midst of them and counted as a spoil 200,150 persons, great and small, male and female, horses, mules, asses, camels, oxen and sheep without number. Hezekiah himself I shut up like a bird in a cage in Jerusalem, his royal city. I built a line of forts against him, and I kept back his heel from going forth out of the great gate of his city. I cut off the cities which I had spoiled from the midst of his land, and gave them to Metinti, king of Ashdod, Padi, king of Ekron, and Zil-baal, king of Gaza, and I made his country small. In addition to their former tribute and yearly gifts I added other tribute and the homage due to my majesty, and I laid it upon them. The fear of the greatness of my majesty overwhelmed him, even Hezekiah, and he sent after me to Nineveh, my royal city, by way of gift and tribute, the Arabs (*Urbi*) and his body-guard whom he had brought for the defence of Jerusalem, his royal city, and had furnished with pay, along with thirty talents of gold, 800 talents of pure silver, carbuncles and other precious stones, a couch of ivory, thrones of ivory, an elephant's hide, an elephant's tusk, rare woods of various names, a vast treasure, as well as the eunuchs of his palace, dancing men and dancing women ; and he sent his ambassador to offer homage.'

INDEX.

LIST OF SCRIPTURE REFERENCES.

www.ingramcontent.com/pod-product-compliance
Lightning Source LLC
Chambersburg PA
CBHW020034030726
47499CB00007B/2424